Jörg Fauser, born in Germany in 1944, was a novelist, essayist and journalist. Having broken his dependency on heroin at the age of thirty, he produced three successful novels, including *The Snowman*, and highly praised essays of literary criticism. On 16 July 1987 he had been out celebrating his forty-third birthday. At dawn, instead of going back to his home, he wandered on to a stretch of motorway, by chance or by choice, and was struck down by a heavy goods lorry. He died instantly.

THE SNOWMAN

Jörg Fauser

Translated from the German by
Anthea Bell

BITTER LEMON PRESS
LONDON

BITTER LEMON PRESS

First published in the United Kingdom in 2004 by
Bitter Lemon Press, 37 Arundel Gardens, London W11 2LW

www.bitterlemonpress.com

First published in German as *Der Schneemann* by
Rogner & Bernhard Verlag, Munich, 1981

The publication of this work was supported by
a grant from the Goethe-Institut.

A CIP record for this book is available from the British Library

ISBN 1–904738–05–2

Typeset by RefineCatch Limited, Broad Street, Bungay, Suffolk
Printed and bound in Great Britain by
Bookmarque Ltd, Croydon, Surrey.

1

Blum looked at his watch. High time to make a move. He drained his coffee cup, took a toothpick out of its plastic container and signalled to the waiter. The bill wasn't enormous – convert it to German currency and it came to no more than five marks – but he'd definitely have to do a deal soon if he was going to afford hot lunches next week. He hated breaking into his emergency funds. He put a couple of cents in his saucer as a tip, and as he left he waved his rolled-up *Times of Malta* to the manager, who was sitting playing cards with the proprietor's daughter. Bright lad. Could be a customer some time soon.

The light was so strong that it momentarily blinded him. He felt for his sunglasses, and just as he realized that he must have left them in the hotel he saw the car that had been constantly in his vicinity for some days, parked beside the carriage pulled by the feeble old white horse. One of the two men in the car now got out and came towards him, a short man with black hair and a suede jacket. The kind of person who never forgets his sunglasses.

"Mr Blum?"

Although he had just had something to drink, his throat felt dry. He took the toothpick out of his mouth.

"Yes?"

"This won't take a moment, sir."

The man opened a wallet and showed his ID, the sort of ID that looks the same all over the world. Blum felt himself breaking out in a sweat. He heard the voice of the retired English major in the newsagent's. Yet again the *Daily Mail* had failed to arrive.

"What's it all about?"

"Inspector Cassar will explain. A mere formality."

"Inspector Cassar? I don't understand. I'm a tourist . . ."

But Blum understood very well, and it was clear that the policeman knew he did. As usual, the major let himself be persuaded to buy the *Daily Telegraph* instead, and Blum threw his toothpick away and followed the police officer to the car. There didn't seem to be anything he could do, not this early in the day.

2

It was a small, stuffy room, but they mostly were. There was a fan in the ceiling, but it was not switched on. Power shortage. The inspector had pushed his chair right back to the wall. His face was in shadow, but Blum had seen enough to know it was not the kind of face you'd want to remember. Neatly parted brown hair, a permanent twitch around the fish-like mouth. His dark suit was faultlessly ironed, and the fingers leafing through Blum's passport were muscular and perfectly manicured. They put the passport aside, looked through a file, and returned to the passport. Maybe they liked its paper better.

"You have a tourist visa valid for one month, Mr Blum."

Inspector Cassar spoke impeccable bureaucrat's English. The bastard, thought Blum. He nodded.

"It expires in three days' time."

"I could have it extended."

"Why would you want to do that?"

"Well, for instance, because I like it so much here on Malta."

"You've already spent a considerable amount of time in these parts, Mr Blum. Rather unusual for a tourist, wouldn't you agree?"

"I know tourists who've been on their travels for years."

"You mean the long-haired sort with their backpacks and guitars? Young people? Oh, come on, Mr Blum, really! If your passport isn't a fake you were born on 29 March 1940. I don't think you can still be regarded as one of the younger generation."

Blum stared at the wall. A fly was inspecting the picture of the President. The man looked more likely to inspire confidence than Inspector Cassar. Maybe that was one reason why he got to be President.

"May I ask what your profession is, Mr Blum?" The inspector's voice still sounded officially distanced and civil, but Blum could hear a harder note in it.

"I'm a businessman, sir."

The inspector moved his chair closer and picked up the file again. "Oh yes. And what kind of business are you in?"

"Most recently I was with an import–export company in Berlin."

"Most recently?"

"Well, the firm wasn't doing too well, so I got my partners to buy me out and then I thought I'd go on vacation for a while. A creative break, you understand."

Inspector Cassar was very close to the desk now, and a strip of sunlight fell over his face. His eyes were yellow. The eyes of a beast of prey. Blum felt his heart thud. He stubbed out his cigarette. His fingers were damp with perspiration.

"For someone in the import–export business you have an unusual vocabulary, Mr Blum. Creative break – garbage! Would you like me to tell you why you fancied this 'creative break'? Because you're a member of an international art theft gang, and you plan to start operating in Morocco and Spain and Tunisia and here in Malta, the way you did back in Istanbul!"

The hard edge that Cassar's tone had assumed reminded Blum of certain particularly self-opinionated schoolteachers he'd known. The inspector lit a Benson

4

& Hedges and blew the smoke over the desk in the direction of Blum's blazer.

"Istanbul? I don't quite understand . . ."

Cassar tapped the file.

"You understand perfectly, Mr Blum. In 1969, according to Interpol, you were part of the organization stealing antique artworks to the tune of over two million dollars from the Izmir Archaeological Museum, including the diadem depicting the twelve labours of Hercules . . ."

Blum cleared his throat.

"Inspector, please allow me to interrupt you, sir. You're bringing up all those slanders that I was able to disprove to the Istanbul police at the time. If Interpol is still making such accusations then they're nothing but totally outlandish rumours and suspicions, and I'd sue if it wouldn't be just a waste of my time."

Cassar forced a smile. "You'd sue Interpol? I must say, Mr Blum, you have quite a nerve!"

"I had nothing to do with it at all! Do you think the Turks would have let me go if they could have shown that I had the slightest connection with the case?"

"Right now I'm not interested in what the Turks did or didn't do." The tone of Cassar's voice was cutting. "If you've been hatching any plans for here, Blum, forget it. Art theft on Malta wouldn't just be against the law of our democratic republic, it would be a direct offence to the Catholic faith of the population, and you couldn't atone for that in a single lifetime."

He threw the file dismissively into the filing cabinet. The fly on the picture crapped on the President's ear. Blum stood up.

"I'm not an art thief, Inspector Cassar."

"Well, whatever your line is, Mr Blum, you won't have much chance to pursue it here. As I said before, your visa runs out in three days' time, and if I were you I wouldn't be too hopeful about getting another. Maybe you can continue your 'creative break' in Italy. The door's over there."

"I shall complain to my ambassador."

"Go ahead, Mr Blum, and good luck. But don't forget, if you're still on Malta an hour after your visa runs out, your ambassador can visit you in Kordin."

"Kordin?"

"Our civil prison, Mr Blum."

3

When the mosquito entered the beam of light from the bedside lamp and began zooming about right in front of the wall, Blum picked up one of the porn magazines and killed it. The wallpaper of the hotel bedroom was spattered with squashed mosquitoes. Blum wiped the magazine on the bedpost and handed it to the Pakistani, who was sitting on the coverlet watching him with eyes older than Pakistan, as old as all that goes on between man, woman and mosquito in the dusk.

"That's life," said Blum. "Hard but fair."

"An interesting thought," said the Pakistani.

Blum took the packet of HB out of his blazer pocket, lit a cigarette and offered the packet to the Pakistani.

"I don't smoke, thanks," he said, smiling, and tipped his head to one side. His skin looked even darker in the dim light. He was wearing a green artificial silk suit and linen shoes, no socks. His long, greasy hair, already touched with grey here and there, lay around his smooth-skinned face like a wreath.

"You're right," said Blum. "Sex is healthier." He looked at his watch. "However, I'm afraid I don't have all day for you, Mr Waq . . ."

"Haq," the Pakistani corrected him. "Hassan Abdul Haq."

"Of course. Mr Haq. Well, what do you think? I'm not sure how much you know about these things, but there's absolutely nothing to equal this old Danish porn."

The Pakistani leafed through the magazines while Blum looked round the room. Category D, he thought, spartan but clean. In summer the old palazzo would probably be quite comfortable, but now, in March, a chill still lingered. And there were mosquitoes all the year round. The Pakistani was travelling light – a small plastic suitcase under the wash-stand, two shirts drying on wire hangers, and magazines and paperbacks which didn't look as if they came from Pakistan on the rickety bedside table. However, Mr Haq had a Remington, and he used expensive aftershave. Blum had travelled lighter himself, and he too couldn't always afford category C.

Mr Haq put the magazine down, looked at Blum with some disappointment, and said, "American products strike me as – how shall I put it? – more realistic."

Blum stubbed out his half-smoked cigarette. The tourists were beginning to sing in the inner courtyard, and he was in a hurry.

"You mean brutal. The Americans are more brutal. Now these are from a time when people still knew how to enjoy each other, if you see what I mean."

Why was he bothering with this? The man probably buggered three sacred cows before breakfast every day. It was crazy anyway, trying to flog porn to Asians.

"What's more, there's nothing else in this line on Malta. So if you want any you'll have to buy mine, Mr Faq. And let me tell you one thing – the Americans will leave your lot in the shit when the Russians come over the Khyber Pass."

"Haq," said the Pakistani, unmoved. "Hassan Abdul Haq. Have you ever been to my country, then?"

No, Mr Blum never had, nor did he intend to go there, not right now. What he saw about it in the newspapers was enough for him.

"Afghanis might get some satisfaction from these products, but in my view they have no artistic merit."

Quite possibly Blum agreed, but no Pakistani was going to tell him so. He picked up a magazine and showed him the best bits.

"These are classics, my dear fellow. Denmark 1968, it's kind of like a vintage wine, know what I mean about vintage wines? Well, no, your sort don't drink, of course. But I can get any price I care to name in Cairo, any price."

However, Mr Haq was not Egyptian, he disapproved of Egyptians on both personal and political grounds, and 1968 meant nothing to him either. He said he thought the magazines were boring. "Always the same woman, always the same man."

"Well, it's always the same game," said Blum. "Maybe the Chinese know a few extra tricks – or the Amazonian Indians, but in itself, as such, it's always the same old thing. Anyway, what do you mean, artistic merit? Who wants artistic merit?"

"American magazines are more interesting."

The Pakistani was staring at a point somewhere over Blum's shoulder. Blum heard a mosquito whining. He's waiting for me to kill that one too, he thought. He likes to have me kill mosquitoes for him. The Paki sits on the bed running down the porn magazines while the white man chases around the room squashing mosquitoes. Some people might think that funny. Not me.

"Maybe you want pictures of two men fisting each other? Or does watching a blonde do it with a pig bring you off? Perhaps you fancy little kids being screwed, Mr Haq?"

Mr Haq looked at Blum as if he were giving this idea profound consideration, and then said, "I could use a man like you, Mr Blum."

9

For a brief, intriguing moment Blum thought the other man was making him a sexual proposition, but then Mr Haq began talking about Saudi Arabia. The people singing in the courtyard struck up "Guantanamera" – three hoarse male and two shrill female voices. Blum was starting to feel he needed a drink.

"I don't want anything to do with Saudi Arabia, Mr Haq. They jail you there for a bottle of whisky. Or give you 100 lashes on the soles of your feet. No thanks!"

"No, no, you can earn good money with whisky. They don't lash you unless you get caught, Mr Blum. And just think of the problem of available sex . . ." The Pakistani seemed to have taken it into his head to enlist this German to help him make his fortune in Saudi Arabia. He told him about the airport built in the middle of the desert sand by German specialists and Pakistani immigrant workers – 15,000 men living in huts, no women and no alcohol, or nothing like enough of either, now wasn't that the kind of golden opportunity that might never come his way again?

"Possibly," said Blum. He stacked the magazines together again. "But I can do okay in Cairo too. Don't you at least want these few? I can give you a good price."

The Pakistani seemed to be waiting for something. Blum did him the favour of killing another mosquito, but Mr Haq clearly had something else in mind. He sat on the bed with his hands folded and stared into the last of the daylight.

"I have good contacts in Jeddah," he said quietly. "One American made a fortune in three months there with watered whisky."

"Maybe he needed it," said Blum.

"And you don't, Mr Blum?"

"Not enough to get mixed up with the Saudis."

"I always knew the Germans were prosperous."

"I must go, Mr Haq."

"Do forgive me for not having offered you anything . . ."

"I'm here to offer *you* something."

"Here, have some of this chocolate. Maltese, but it doesn't taste bad."

Finally Mr Haq deigned to buy two magazines, but he haggled over fifty cents so long that when Blum closed the door he had a bitter taste in his mouth, and not just because he was thirsty.

4

Even when business was bad or deportation threatened, Blum allowed himself a good dinner in an agreeable bar at least once a week, and in Malta he had chosen Thursdays for this purpose. On Thursdays they had a curry night in the Pegasus Bar of the Phoenicia Hotel. Blum liked the place – a hotel in the colonial British style, a bar decorated with fake medieval weapons, a sarong-clad waitress on duty specially for the curry night, Englishmen in the textiles industry who sighed and had second helpings of everything, and American tourists tearing their President to shreds after the third bourbon. The dollar was at rock bottom again.

Mr Hackensack did not hold forth about the President. Nor was he a tourist.

"I'm a loyal American citizen," he said, having lit his Davidoff. "A patriot. Just so long as no one catches him selling the White House silver spoons to the Russians, the President's above suspicion, that's the way I see it."

Hackensack was a corpulent man of around sixty who squeezed his bulky body into check suits much too small for him, and planted excessively colourful hats on his massive head. The rolls of flesh on his chin and cheeks compressed his mouth so that its pursed lips made it look curiously small and delicate. There were flashy rubies set in solid gold on the middle and ring fingers of his left hand, and a matching tie-pin glittered in his spotted tie. Blum had often had a drink with Hackensack before, but only this evening did the American let slip that he himself had worked for the government.

"You were with the CIA?"

Hackensack's face assumed an affected smile.

"I'd once have felt flattered to be asked if I was with the Firm, but nowadays . . ."

"I hope I didn't insult you. I don't know a lot about these secret service affairs. What you don't know won't make trouble for you, that's my philosophy."

Hackensack laughed, but it was only his rolls of fat creasing up. His eyes were not laughing. Blum felt he was being sized up, but that was Americans for you, and Hackensack seemed to need someone to talk to. He ordered another two drinks. The textiles trade mingled with the tourist trade in the Pegasus Bar, and the Maltese godfathers sat in the corner in their black suits, watching the boxing on TV. Blum's policemen friends couldn't find him here. Inspector Cassar's expense account probably didn't stretch to more than a lemonade at the kiosk over by the bus station. The curry was being cleared away. While Hackensack explained to him why power was not just the salt of life but its very essence, Blum looked the women tourists over, but there was no one here today who seemed a hopeful prospect for him, and as she took the dishes away the beauty in the sarong was billing and cooing with the chef, a man weighing two hundredweight from the Weser Mountains who had cooked for the specialist supply troops in Saigon. Hackensack raised his glass and cleared his throat.

"Why so thoughtful, Blum? Business in a bad way, or has someone gone off with your girl?"

The American's nose was beginning to glow, and his cauliflower ears had a rosy tinge. But the bourbon left his eyes cold. He had said he came from Tennessee, but Blum didn't think he was really a southerner.

"In a bad way is about right, Mr Hackensack."

"What, and you a German?"

Blum was tired of this. Did the whole world think all Germans were winners because Hitler had lost the war?

"Not every German is a millionaire just because the mark is strong, Mr Hackensack."

"Call me Harry. Yes, I know, Blum. My firm has a branch in Frankfurt. Drop in when you have business there."

Blum took the card and put it in his wallet.

"I don't expect to be in Frankfurt in the near future, but thanks all the same. What line of business are you in, if I may ask, or does that come under the heading of state secrets?"

Hackensack spluttered, swallowed the wrong way, and went purple. In his tight suit with his sweaty little hat on his head, he now looked like a boxing manager who hasn't had a winner on his books for ten years. Probably just a poor sap like the rest of us, thought Blum.

"I'm a company adviser," said Hackensack, when he had got his breath back. "And if I were to advise *you* some day you'd get a discount – after all, both of us here on Malta, that counts for something."

"I'm only a one-man firm, but if I do need advice I'll be happy to get in touch. Another drink? The next round's on me."

Naturally Hackensack would like another drink. He tipped bourbon down his throat like water with no obvious effect, except that the broken veins of his nose took on a darker hue.

"What lines of business would you say are on the up now?" asked Blum.

"Anything to do with power," said Hackensack, wiping the sweat from his neck with a red flowered handkerchief, which deprived his words of much of their force. "Naked, profitable power with no regard for human feelings, Herr Blum. Of course that's nothing new, as you must know yourself. You Germans have thought a good deal about it too, but you always see the problem in an abstract light, too metaphysically. Power is something concrete, like the whiskey in this glass and its effects."

What nonsense, thought Blum – I could be with a woman somewhere, or trying to flog those porn magazines, and instead I sit here listening to what this jerk has to say about power, which is nothing very new. But what *was* new? His own story, his dreams and failures were nothing new either. Perhaps he might yet find out whether the old fellow was simply feeding him sugar lumps like a monkey for no good reason, or whether there was any point to all this talk.

"So right now I'd say information is big business. And anything that alters the structure of the little grey cells, of course. Chemicals, Mr Blum. Yessir, chemicals are really big business. Combine information with chemicals and the world's your oyster."

"I don't see much chance for me to get a foot in the door," replied Blum. "I mean, it's rather too late in the day to start in that line . . ."

Hackensack looked hard at Blum, and said, before raising the cigar to his delicate lips, "It's never too late. You just need the right attitude, my dear fellow, then you'll always fall on your feet. Take me – I've come a cropper many a time, from the Korean War to Berlin and south-east Asia, and I've always fallen on my feet. You have to in my line of business."

"I thought you were a company adviser."

"An adviser, man, let's just say an adviser."

Blum wasn't about to insist on knowing the difference, nor did he want to spend any more time with this sweating colossus, who was beginning to strike him as bogus. He was getting on Blum's nerves. Information, chemicals, south-east Asia – all very well, but what would Hackensack say if Blum told him about Inspector Cassar? He'd better get moving. He was just wondering how to shake Hackensack off when he saw a woman tourist who had come into the Pegasus alone, and was now standing at the bar looking rather helpless. She was tall and thin and short-sighted, and wore a flowered dress and a knitted jacket. She was no beauty queen but she might save the day. He waved to the barkeeper, and showed his remarkably good teeth when he smiled at her.

"I think you must be from Germany too," he said, turning away from Hackensack.

5

A male cockroach grabbed a female of the species with its forelegs and mounted her. When they had slid over to the title of the "Don't Go Breaking My Heart" track, Blum put a coin in the slot of the jukebox, pressed the button and watched the cockroaches mating. The jukebox was full of cockroaches dead and alive. Rock freaks, thought Blum. Dancing on the machine's hot electric belly, rocking and screwing themselves to death. Have fun, you two. The cockroach let go of the female. She slid over "Sailing" and "La Barca" and lay motionless on "Please Don't Go". Her lover had killed her. With scorpions it's the female, with cockroaches the male. That's life, girlie. Blum picked up his beer and looked out at the street again where, to the roar of the music, young girls on the make were lying in wait for tourists who were just wondering whether to allow themselves a half-bottle of wine at lunch, or buy their wives the T-shirt saying "I lost my heart in Malta".

Finally Larry turned up. Larry was an Australian who had lost a lung in Vietnam. Since then he had been drawing a monthly pension from the Australian government and drinking it away in the cheaper seaports of southern Europe. The number of cheaper seaports was reduced by one every year. He was a thin fellow with a leathery face and a beard sprinkled with grey, and he wore the same faded windcheater every day. He knew his way around boats, and his papers described his profession as soldier.

"Come on, Blum," he said, having overcome his coughing fit with a Scotch. "The wop's waiting for you."

"Is he going to buy them?"

"He wants to see a sample."

They took one of the green buses where the drivers' cabs are decked out like household altars with pink-cheeked Virgins, soulful Sons of God, garlands of plastic flowers and biblical quotations in Latin. They sat wedged between farmers and schoolgirls and English married couples. These last smelled of vermouth and were chewing beans or sucking sweets. The husbands were telling each other old jokes – "Heard the one about the Sikh who wanted to emigrate to Canada?" – and their wives were casting moist-eyed glances at the young Maltese men from behind their colourful travel brochures. Blum envied them. It was a few years yet before he'd be their age, but here he was already among them, and he didn't know any jokes, nor did he have moist eyes, only an old porn magazine in his bag. And if he wasn't gone in a couple of days the cops would be down on him. What kept him going? The same as kept the bus going: fuel and faith, the fuel in his case being spirits. *Verbum dei caro factum est,* said the motto on the cab in front, which as far as he could remember meant: God's word was made flesh.

Well, there must be a soup pan somewhere, then, to help feed the desperados among us.

The tourists got out in Mosta. The men already had damp patches on their polo shirts, and the women's armpit hair was shining wetly.

"Plenty of gold here," said Blum, glancing at the church, which was showy in the Maltese neo-Baroque style.

"Only a fool would try it," replied Larry. "Rob a church on Malta? Something like nicking Lenin's corpse from its mausoleum in Red Square. That's where they keep it, right?"

Blum jumped. "Ever tangled with the police here, Larry?"

"What would make you think that?"

The bus rattled on, and Blum leaned back and pretended not to have heard the question. Just coincidence, he thought. Beyond Mosta the farming country began – dry soil from which the farmers conjured fruit and vegetables with the water that fell in the rainy season. Now the almond trees were in blossom, there was a scent of fruit and flowers, wind and the sea and women. Blum leaned his head against the window and closed his eyes, and for a moment abandoned himself to the illusion of something that would never really be – peace, happiness, magic . . . Then he opened his eyes again, saw the Australian coughing up the mucus from his lungs, and a squinting girl in a blue school uniform who had been watching him all this time and now blushed and looked ahead of her again. He took the Moroccan shades with the gold-rimmed lilac lenses out of his jacket pocket and put them on. These things were worth their price. Sometimes they reduced even the Med to tolerable dimensions.

They got out at the harbour in St Paul's Bay. The little place lay quiet in the sun. A yapping dog chased the bus. Two German tourists shouldered their gigantic backpacks outside a café with a curtain of plastic strips over its doorway. Somewhere an electric lawnmower was stuttering, and a farmer was driving a donkey out into the fields. The windows of the houses did not look out on the street. They walked slowly along the quay. Larry pointed out a motor-boat tied up a little way from the others.

"That's Rossi's boat. A Bertram 32-footer with twin V8 diesel engines, all tuned up like a high-class tart. You could shake any coastguard off in that boat."

"Why would he want to do that?"

"Why do you think, mate?"

Larry lit his twentieth Rothman King Size of the day and spat a mouthful of mucus out into the water of the harbour without getting his cigarette wet.

"What would he smuggle around here? Church altars?"

"Not dried vegetables, that's for sure. Come on, he'll be in his palazzo now blow-drying his perm."

The Villa Aurora was the last house in a cul-de-sac. Judging by its exterior, Rossi's smuggling business couldn't be in a very flourishing state. A palm tree was decaying among empty petrol cans in the front garden, it was a long time since the pink colourwash of the walls had been freshened up, and the plaster over the door was crumbling. When Larry pressed the bell Blum saw a curtain briefly drawn aside in the house next door. The bell rang faintly. Somewhere inside a dog began barking. When the door opened the curtain in the window of the house next door fell back into place again. An old woman in black said something in Maltese, and Blum was surprised to hear Larry answering her in the same language. That made him suspicious. The woman disappeared, and was replaced by a Great Dane that stood staring at the strangers with bloodshot eyes. Then Rossi appeared, whistled the dog to him, and showed them in.

The room into which the Italian led them looked out on the garden and was pleasantly cool. Here too the walls needed a new coat of plaster, but the furnishings were comfortable, and pictures of Maltese and Arab scenes gave the dimly lit place a touch of luxury. In the garden Blum saw a blonde beauty, a real pin-up, sun-bathing stark naked on a lounger. He had some dif-ficulty in taking his eyes off her. Blondes did that to him. Finally he took the glass the Italian was offering him.

"I take it you drink tequila."

"Mm. Viva Zapata."

Rossi had a soft, hoarse voice, and after the first sip of his margarita Blum saw that Larry had not been exaggerating about the perm. The Italian's long black hair tumbled in elaborate ringlets over his shoulders and his close-fitting silk shirt, which was open to the navel to reveal a bronzed chest. The man's face, how-ever, was anything but softly undulating. It was a brown crag with two hard eyes and a brutal chin. Blum put him in his early thirties. After the third sip he won-dered what this man needed porn magazines for. But Rossi was already coming to the point. His English was as fluent as Blum's own, and he spoke with a slight American accent.

"Got one of your mags with you? Let's have a look."

He leafed through it with the air of an expert, his gold bracelets clinking.

"Yup, just as lousy as I expected. But tell you what, I have a customer with a liking for this kind of thing."

"An Arab?"

Rossi's glance suggested that he had considerable stocks of malice in reserve. "Could be he's a German, Blum."

"Why not?" said Blum, shrugging his shoulders.

"How many of these do you have?"

"There's a couple of hundred left."

"Sold some here already?"

"A man's got to live."

"And you really make a living from these – these magazines?"

"I take what comes. I don't see it as any more immoral than selling Coca-Cola. Or tequila."

"I meant can you live on it? After all, these magazines are rather – well, shall we say outdated?"

"There's always a customer to be found somewhere, right?"

The Italian laughed. When he laughed he didn't look so uncongenial, perhaps because his teeth were rather bad. In other circumstances Blum might have laughed too. But his situation was both too ridiculous and too desperate for him to laugh it off. He drank his margarita instead. Larry pretended to be looking at the pictures. The pin-up girl was now lying on her stomach, and the Great Dane sat beside her, ears pricked, staring at the house.

"Right, now about the price. Here, have another. Margarita, the dealers' drink, okay? Because you're a dealer too, my dear fellow, am I right? We're all dealers, even Larry here's a dealer, isn't that so, Larry?"

The Australian coughed, wiped his mouth, stared at the backs of his hands and then said, "It's your party, Rossi."

Rossi laughed and poured something into his own glass. Blum suspected it was pure lemonade.

"Of course," said Rossi. "I'm always throwing parties. I love parties. Like to come to my next party, Blum? But come on, tell me your price, *avanti*. I'm in a hurry."

He made an obscene gesture in the direction of the garden. Blum named his price. Rossi looked horrified.

"That's crazy! Six hundred dollars – why, that's three dollars a copy! *Mamma mia*, I guess you don't know your market . . ."

But Blum wasn't going to be beaten down. There was Cairo, there was a Pakistani bulk purchaser who supplied to Saudi Arabia. No, $600 was a fair price.

"And don't forget, these things are classics in their way. Like a vintage wine. Copenhagen 1968 – well, there's not many of those left. Look at this, Björn Söderbaum's 'Spring Awakening' series, what d'you think that would fetch in Hong Kong? Söderbaum, a genius in his field. Here, this is where he used the camera's-eye technique for the first time – the three-dimensional perspective – I'll have all China standing in line for these if I take them there."

Rossi stepped back and narrowed his eyes, but not in order to appreciate Söderbaum's artistry better.

"I thought I had your measure, Blum. Three-dimensional perspective, *porca Madonna*. Okay, 500 dollars, and perhaps we'll do business again some time."

"Five hundred and fifty, Rossi, and that's my last word. And I'll need a deposit of 100 dollars, or I'll do the deal with the Pakistani after all."

But Rossi had no dollars around the place, and after much haggling they agreed on forty Maltese pounds. Rossi counted the money out.

"Bring me the magazines to the Phoenicia at eleven this evening. Room 523. Then there's something else we might discuss."

He winked at Blum and jerked his chin in the direction of Larry, who had now finished with the pictures and was inspecting the bottles in the home bar. Blum nodded and put the money away. As they left, he took a final look at the garden. Rossi's girl was already immersed in the porn magazine, and even the Great Dane was showing an interest in Söderbaum's brilliant technique in "Spring Awakening".

As they stood by the juke box again in the Playgirl later, Blum said, "Do you think he's really buying the magazines for a customer?"

The jungle of Da Nang could already be seen in Larry's eyes, and he simply shrugged his shoulders.

"Of course you get the extra fifty dollars I wangled out of him, mate. Now I just have to pay the hotel bill."

"Did I ever tell you how they dropped us off by mistake in the area they'd saturated with poison gas the day before?"

As Larry tried to exorcize the horrors that he could never drive out of his mind, Blum watched the cockroaches copulating and sliding all over the titles of the discs. The music droned out its horror songs, and Blum had difficulty keeping everything straight in his mind, horror on one side, lust on the other, his own memories. But in the end those memories of his always won out against other people's horror or lust: his own memories, the nastiest on earth.

6

But never mind, thought Blum that evening in his
room by the harbour, you have to make it – you're not
Larry, you're not an Australian, you didn't breathe
poison gas in Vietnam, you're Blum and you have to
make it, all you need is a chance, just one real chance,
the big fish, the jackpot, no more cheap tricks then,
just to be rolling in the dough, oh Lord, bringing in
the real loot, get your head up out of the dirt, see the
real hot sun, *Madonna mia*, and when they bring the
bill you can sign it in style.

He leafed through the book he had bought in
November from an American in Algeciras. It was the
Bahamas Handbook and Businessman's Annual, Nassau
1978, with a foreword by the governor-general. A
photograph showed him: Sir John Cash with the
Queen. A handsome black man with mischief in his
face. Fair enough, a joke was a joke, and there was a
quirkiness about the Bahamas anyway – but a country
where the man in charge was actually called Cash, well,
that was something else. The American had asked
Blum what his line of business was, and Blum had
smiled vaguely and said the construction industry.
That always sounded good. So what did he himself
do, he had asked the American. Oh, he worked for the
government, the man had replied with an equally
vague smile, looking at Blum as if expecting an insult.
But Blum nodded understandingly and looked to see
how big a tip the Yank would give. None, of course.

Blum looked at the photographs of members of the Bahamian parliament. Most of them were black, belonged to the Progressive Liberal Party, and were either businessmen or trade unionists or both. If he was in the construction industry, the American had said as they parted, the Bahamas would suit him nicely, the place was in the middle of the biggest building boom in the Western hemisphere. That was another odd thing, a man who worked for the government offering a book that was probably handed out to every tourist, selling it to him for two dollars. Well, the Yanks probably needed it now. Even Hackensack with his Havanas and his bourbon and the rubies on his sausage fingers needed something or other, you could tell. Blum, who had seen many booms come and go, almost declined to buy the book, but now he was glad he had. There were days when even the import–export statistics and the estate agents' ads, not to mention the chapter on the flora of the Bahamas (it was nice to know they grew cauliflowers there too), acted on him like a pain-killer, lulling him, carrying him away to eternally sunny beaches where there were palm trees and flying fish, and women with garlands of flowers welcomed visitors. But Blum was never one of those visitors. Blum did not feature in these dreams at all, and that was the best thing about them – he was in no danger of any disappointments.

A knock. As he went to the door he looked at the time. He had to set off for Rossi's. He must have fallen asleep.

"I hope I'm not disturbing you," said Mr Haq, flashing a gold tooth at Blum. He was still wearing his green artificial silk suit, but for this visit he had put on black plastic shoes and even socks. For all his solicitude he made an impression of determination, like a man who has geared himself up to demanding a rise.

"I'm afraid I have to go straight off to meet some-one," said Blum, tucking his shirt into his trousers. He too washed his own shirts, and yet again the good navy-blue shirt from Tangiers was rather crumpled because he had been lying around in it.

"Oh, I won't keep you long," said the Pakistani, cast-ing a quick glance around the room. What he saw seemed to satisfy him. So the German was no better off than he was. "I was hoping you'd come and see me again and give me a chance to . . ."

"The magazines are all sold, Mr Haq. I'm just taking them to the buyer."

"I wasn't thinking of the magazines, Mr Blum."

The blood rose to Blum's head. All he needed now was an exhaustive discussion of the problems of those 15,000 Pakistani immigrant workers in the desert between Mecca and Jeddah. Why did losers always latch on to him? He went over to the wash-basin and combed his hair. A cockroach crawled into the waste pipe, but only as a matter of form. Blum glanced in the mirror. Now his hair was thinning at the sides too. He supposed the day would soon come when he had more hope than hair. But the Pakistani was not among his hopes – not yet.

"Mr Haq, if you're thinking of your Saudi Arabian dreams . . ."

"Oh, not dreams, Mr Blum! They're concrete ideas – more than ideas, they're plans!"

Blum washed his hands. The towel was still last week's.

"Mr Haq, I'm leaving in the next few days. But Jeddah is not on my route."

"May I ask where you're going?"

Blum put his jacket on.

"I haven't fixed the details yet, but I'm thinking of Italy."

"Italy? Mr Blum, do you know Italy?" He put a sweet in his mouth, showing two gold teeth. "Why not discuss my plans at our leisure? What would a man like you do in Italy? They don't even have proper money there."

Blum lit his cigarette and took the case full of magazines out of the wardrobe. That was it for now.

"Money's money, Mr Haq. Italian money is money too. And I expect I'll make a little detour to Germany – my own country, as you know. There's a lot to be done there, as we say at home. We'll see what we can do about it."

The Pakistani nodded, and looked from the case back to Blum. He had to raise his head to do so.

"I've been there myself. In fact my Saudi plans take in a trip to West Germany . . ."

Blum picked up the case. "I tell you what, Mr Haq – why not look in again tomorrow, and then I'll tell you just why I'm not interested."

"Not interested? How can you say you're not interested before you know what my plans are?"

"I'm relying on instinct. Come on, I have to get moving."

The Pakistani gave a melancholy smile. "I'd hoped you were an open-minded man, someone who could discuss the problems of modern life – and after that a business relationship usually develops of itself."

Then he was out in the corridor at last, and Blum could lock the door of his room.

"All in good time, Mr Haq. I'll be happy to tell you a thing or two about the problems of modern life once I know I can pay my hotel bill."

The Pakistani said no more. They went down the dimly lit stairs and out into the street. Blum inhaled the mingled smells of refuse and the fragrance of flowers. The refuse was winning. From the harbour came the howl of a ship's siren. Blum lit an HB and turned to the Pakistani, whose face was grotesquely discoloured under the red light of the hotel sign.

"Good night, Mr Haq."

"I could really use a man like you, Mr Blum."

Oh no you couldn't, thought Blum, quickly walking up the street. At the next corner he looked back at the Pakistani once more. Mr Haq was still standing under the red light, and it looked to Blum as if he were signalling to someone on the other side of the street. This character is beginning to get me down, he thought.

Republic Street was still very busy. Faces of all ethnic groups, rock music from the discos, neon lighting. Blum used his case to clear himself a way through the crowd. A small boy tugged at his sleeve.

"Mister! Hey, mister!"

The same old story. Blum went on. The boy was not giving up; he showed him something. A small picture. Oh no, thought Blum, here comes the competition. The priests, those bastards, using kids to do their work for them.

"For the Church, mister!"

Blum stopped and was immediately pushed to one side by the crowd. A Japanese made way for him, giving him an encouraging smile, as if to say: Go on, make the best of it.

"For the Church? Let's have a look."

The urchin handed him the picture and Blum looked at it, his case jammed between his feet. The Virgin Mary, wearing a blue robe and surrounded by dark clouds, stood on the terrestrial globe with her arms outstretched, a circlet of little stars above her head. She was smiling tenderly. No, there was really nothing she could do for this vale of tears here below. There was wording in Maltese on the back. *Madonna berikni u salvani.* You didn't need to know the language to get the general idea. The urchin tugged Blum's sleeve.

"For the Church, mister!"

If Inspector Cassar could see me now, thought Blum gloomily, fumbling in his trouser pocket for small change. At the same moment someone pushed him from behind and then held him hard against the window of a bookshop. It all happened very fast – a sudden jerk, and when he had freed himself he realized that his case was gone. The boy was gone too, and Blum was left holding the little picture of the Virgin Mary. The crowd surged indifferently by. The bells of St John's Cathedral rang. It was eleven o'clock.

7

The key was in the door of room 523, and the wooden tag with the room number was still swinging slightly from its ring, as if the door had only just been closed. Blum knocked quietly.

"Rossi? Are you there, Rossi?"

No answer. Blum was sure no one had seen him enter the hotel. A middle-aged man with lilac shades, a blazer and a cravat was as natural a sight in these surroundings as a drunken seaman in Strait Street. All the same, he felt he was being watched. Someone had been following him all the time. Someone who'd rather steal a case full of old Danish porn magazines than pay $550 for them. The lift clicked shut and glided down. Of course the inspector was capable of anything. Why just the inspector? Anyone was capable of anything. Blum knocked again. Nothing moved. The lift was down at the ground floor now. Blum had no choice – he entered the room. Whoever had closed the door had done so not as he came into the room but as he left it, and had then left the key in the lock. And if this had been the scene of Blum's "next party", then Blum was glad to have missed it. The elegant room was totally devastated. The mattresses had been slit open, and their stuffing looked almost as unappetizing as the sandwiches sticking to the walls and the dark puddles on the carpet, which was covered with broken bottles and smashed glasses. Whoever had been wreaking such havoc in this crowded hotel with its swarms of tourists and gala evenings, its big receptions and dozens of security men, whoever had taken the time to smash glazed picture frames, turn bedside tables into match-wood, tear the sunblinds down from the window and pull out the telephone, must have been one of the actors in the drama. But on what stage? And what was the play? And how did he himself and his pathetic porn magazines feature in it? Was he just an extra or one of the main characters in the cast? He glanced at the window. Not a bad view. This small, floodlit rock in the Mediterranean, a fold in the scarf over the Madonna's head, *for the Church*, yes, sure, but . . . everything was crammed so close out there, everyone knew everyone else, and he, Blum, had thought he could keep himself to himself here and lead a cushy life. Ha, ha. He wondered where the jail was – what was its name again? Kordin. Probably further off, in the pitch dark.

And where might Signor Rossi be?

Not in the wardrobe, anyway, since curiously enough that was completely empty, as if no one were staying here at all, nor in the bathtub, and not under the bed either. Or was he? Wasn't that Rossi's hair? Blum had a queasy feeling in the pit of his stomach. Suppose the police storm into this room, and here I am, known in town as an art thief and porn dealer, with Rossi's corpse under the bed – *Madonna salvani*. Well, what could he do about it? He bent down for a closer look. What he saw surprised him, confronting him with a mystery, but at least his stomach signalled the all clear. It wasn't Rossi's corpse under the bed, only Rossi's hair. Without really wanting to, Blum put his hand out and picked the hair up. It hadn't been cut off, it was a wig. Really, what a jerk! Those glorious tumbling locks all artificial, 30,000 lire in a department store. He turned the wig over to look at the net lining, and his queasy feeling instantly returned. There was a strip of sticky tape on the inner band, and if you looked closely you could see a piece of paper under it. He took a deep breath and pulled away the sticky tape.

A note, carefully folded six times. Blum unfolded it just as carefully. A receipt from the left luggage office at Munich Central Station, counter 1, dated 2 February 1980. The receipt bore the number 55 601. Rather worn, but no red wine stains on it, no spaghetti sauce, everything okay and valid. Blum stood there in the wrecked room for a few moments frowning, smelling nothing, seeing nothing, hearing nothing, thinking nothing. Then he folded the receipt up again and put it in the breast pocket of his jacket, with the red hand-kerchief, the book of matches from the Pegasus Bar, and the picture of the Madonna that had cost him $550 and maybe a good deal more.

Steps passed by outside, laughter, a door somewhere was opened and slammed shut. Then Blum was in the lift, smoothing back his hair, and with his lilac shades, his cravat, his height of 5 feet 10 inches from head to foot he was very much the old, carefree Blum on field duty, always with a knowing smile on his lips, just a hint of haste as he made his way to the bar, lighting the inevitable cigarette outside the swing doors, and once inside his first glance was for the women at the bar. This was the high life.

"You look like you just met Lady Macbeth," said Hackensack, moving up to make room for Blum beside him.

"Thanks, don't bother," said Blum. He had seen a woman he knew, and Hackensack's nose was purple yet again.

"You didn't meet Lady Macbeth? Then maybe the ghost of Hamlet's father?"

"Mr Hackensack," said Blum, "I might well call in on you in Frankfurt after all. Will you be there next week?"

"You do just that," said Hackensack. His fat jowls drooped over his chin, but his eyes were like violets on ice. He brought the flat of his hand down on the bar. "Frankfurt! What a city! Always something to be had there. Would you like a bourbon, or what's the matter with you? Turned Holy Joe, eh?" He laughed like someone who was being paid for it, and Blum straightened his shades and pushed past him to the woman he had recognized. She was married to a dentist in Düsseldorf.

"Why, hello there, darling," she said, digging her long nails into his wrist. Blum flinched. His stomach was still giving him cause for concern. He stared at the doorway. Larry had suddenly appeared in his windcheater, and stood there stroking his chin.

"You're in dead trouble," said Larry, once Blum was out of the bar. Buses clattered across the square to the City Gate, backfiring. A strong wind had risen.

"You can say that again," said Blum. "Someone stole my case with the mags in it."

"That fits. I reckon Rossi's mixed up with something that's not gone down too well with the other side. And seems like, to Rossi, you look like one of them."

"So who is the other side, then?"

Larry shrugged his shoulders and flicked his cigarette end away.

"Look, don't start stonewalling . . ."

"Not so loud," said the Australian. "I don't know who the other side is. Does it matter? In Vietnam —"

"We're not in Vietnam, Larry. Someone's stolen 550 dollars from me, 50 of which were going to be yours, that's the point. And don't try telling me fairytales about the Maltese Mafia."

The door of the bar opened and the woman from Düsseldorf tottered out on her platform heels.

"Where are you, darling? Don't you like your little Helga any more? Hey, you there, no running off with my Blum!"

She babbled on at random, making no sense. You're done for, Blum told himself, you're all washed up here on Malta – with a dentist's drunk wife on your arm, a left-luggage receipt from Munich Central in your pocket, stolen out of a wig worn by a wop to whom you were planning to flog 200 porn magazines, and an Australian with only one lung who can't shake off his nightmares there among the palms in front of you. Not to mention Inspector Cassar wiping his arse on your old Interpol file . . . although not until you've pushed off. Robbed, washed up, threatened on all sides, allow me to introduce myself, Blum of the construction industry, just waiting for the boom to revive my own fortunes too. Suddenly he felt how cold it had turned.

"Come along, darling, let's have another!"

Blum freed himself for the second time, left the woman and went off with Larry towards the City Gate. The dentist's wife was shouting after him.

"I'll take you to Gozo," said Larry. "You'll be safe from your girlfriend there."

"Gozo?" Blum stopped. "What would I do on Gozo? Grow tomatoes?"

"Only trying to be helpful, mate. After all, I got you into this shit with Rossi."

"Come off it, Larry. I've never had any trouble getting myself into the shit."

They had reached the City Gate, where the stalls were closing down for the night. The Australian stared at Blum, whose eyes showed nothing.

"What're you going to do now, then?"

Blum compressed his lips. What he was going to do was no business of anyone else, not even an Australian who wanted to help him.

"See you some time."

"Blum, wait!"

But Blum had already turned the corner.

8

After the taxi had rattled through Munich for half an eternity, Blum tapped the driver on the shoulder.

"This your first day on the job, is it?"

"Here we are, boss," said the driver, stepping on the brake. Blum got out. It was perishing cold, but at least it wasn't snowing. The hotel was called the Metropol. He saw one wing of Munich Central Station opposite. The cab driver gave him change of 70 marks from a 100-mark note. Now he had just 170 marks, 25 dirham and 5 Maltese pounds. A porter offered to take his bag, but Blum waved him away. Then he had an idea.

"There's something waiting for me in left luggage. Could you fetch it? I've been flying for sixteen hours. I'm done in."

"Of course, sir. At your service."

Blum gave the porter the left-luggage receipt. During the flight from Frankfurt he had unfolded it and smoothed it out. The porter disappeared into the night with it. Blum went to the reception desk and asked about rooms. There was one vacant, DM 106 with bath and breakfast. He registered. In the box against "Profession" he wrote "Manager". Then he looked around him. The lobby was spacious. A flight of steps led up to the restaurant in the gallery, which had a glass roof over it. Thick carpets, lots of crystal chandeliers, genuine fifties décor. He could hear the enticing clink of glasses from the bar at the far end of the lobby, and the hoarse voice of an intoxicated woman, but Blum felt nervous and knew it would show. Either the Mafia would storm into the hotel next minute, or the porter was lying on the floor of the left-luggage office clutching his hands to a hole in his belly.

The clerk at reception had never taken his eyes off Blum. Now he cleared his throat and asked, "Where did you say you've just come from?"

Blum had said nothing about it at all. Now he replied, without thinking, "Rio."

"I thought as much," said the clerk. "I recognize the symptoms."

"What symptoms?"

"Jetlag, effects of the climate change. It makes people all overwrought. I recommend a warm bath, not too hot because of the metabolism. It's still winter here, you know."

Blum tried to smile, nodded, and lit a cigarette. Winter, *porca Madonna.* It had been snowing in Frankfurt, and when he spent twenty minutes standing in the spotlight in front of the security machine because his bag had been picked out for checking he felt like turning straight back. But not to return to Malta. The two hours he had to spend in the Luqa airport restaurant, because of course there were delays on Air Malta, were among those experiences he could happily have done without and would never forget. Sweating with terror, hands trembling, heart failure threatening every time someone looking even remotely Italian came into the restaurant . . . Blum had realized that almost all the Maltese could look Italian.

How much longer was the porter going to take? Blum fought down his stomach cramps. The clerk was still loafing about behind the reception desk, and now the telephonist was watching him too, so he withdrew to the back of the lobby and finally ended up in the bar. Two Arabs in made-to-measure suits were sitting in a corner seat, conversing in low tones. The hoarse-voiced woman had the bar to herself.

"I won," she told the barkeeper triumphantly. "He came in."

The barkeeper looked at Blum, shrugging his shoulders. "What'll it be?"

"You mean me?"

The woman laughed. She was wearing a canary-yellow trouser suit which made her blonde hair look pale. She was perhaps no more than thirty-five, but the drink had already ravaged her face, and there was nothing make-up could do for it now. But her voice was so sexy that Blum felt a tug between his thighs.

"We had a bet," she told him. "I saw you out in the lobby, and I told Tito here, I bet he'll be here in the bar in three minutes' time ordering a schnapps, am I right, Tito?"

"Don't call me Tito," said the Yugoslavian. Then he looked impatiently at Blum. "A beer, maybe?"

"A cognac," said Blum.

"Okay, this round's on Tito," said the woman. She took a cigarette out of a case and leaned towards Blum for a light, holding his wrist. She wore expensive-looking jewellery. The varnish was flaking off her fingernails, and her perfume smelled a little stale too.

"So how did you know I'd come into the bar?"

"I know the symptoms, darling."

Blum almost choked on his cognac. Maybe the Germans had gone out of their minds while he was away and now spent their time sitting in hotel lobbies, pinpointing other people's symptoms.

"You really did need that cognac, see?"

"True," said Blum. "I'm just back from the Amazon. I've had nothing to drink there for a year but liana wine."

She liked that. She looked at Blum as if ready to fall into his arms any minute. Blum moved slightly away.

"So what were you doing there? Teaching the Indians how to speculate on the stock market? My last husband did that so well they're letting him give courses on it in Stadelheim. You know what Stadelheim is?"

Blum nodded, and glanced at the time. He'd give the porter three more minutes.

"Yes, he was a good con man, my Fritzi, but he conned me best of all. Do they have con men in Amazonia?"

"Of course. The con trick rules the world."

"You say that so – so casually. Well, how do you like Germany these days?"

"It's overwhelming. In every way," said Blum.

"Doing anything this evening?"

Her glance was so desperate that Blum felt fear. This really was one fear too many.

"Yes, I have to meet some business colleagues."

"Here you are, sir," said the porter at this moment, putting a carton down on the bar stool next to Blum. The carton had a red and white label on it saying "Old Spice Shaving Foam".

"Oh, so *that's* your line of business," said the blonde, looking away, suddenly bored. Blum paid the porter, picked up the carton and carried it to the lift, his face red, and in the lift he wondered what line of business she meant – sales rep, pharmacist or simply a poor sap? His face in the lift mirror showed nothing but bafflement. Probably a combination of all three, he thought. A poor sap who works as sales rep for a pharmacist.

9

When he reached room 316 he put the carton down on the bed, took off his jacket, turned up the central heating, glanced out of the window and drew the curtain.

Shaving foam.

Old Spice shaving foam.

A carton full of Old Spice shaving foam in the left-luggage office of Munich Central. The receipt stuck inside the wig of an Italian allegedly called Rossi, last seen on 13 March in the Villa Aurora, St Paul's Bay, Malta. Malta, an island state in the Mediterranean, halfway between Sicily and Africa, form of government "democratic republic", faith Roman Catholic, right, Inspector? Population 320,000, exports early spring vegetables, Mediterranean fruits, immigrant workers, cleaning ladies. And no art treasures. A smuggler's boat, Larry had said. To smuggle Old Spice shaving foam? Where to? Jeddah? Mr Faq might have considered even that good business. Sorry, Mr *Haq*. Hassan Abdul Haq. *Madonna salvani.* He opened the carton.

Old Spice shaving foam. Not a doubt about it. Twenty jumbo cans of Old Spice shaving foam, 10 fl oz net, from the firm of Shulton, New York – London – Paris. He read the printed wording: "CAUTION: Pressurized cans. Do not heat above 122°F (keep out of direct sunlight). After use do not force open or burn. Do not spray on naked flames or heated bodies." That sounded

41

ominous. What did they mean, heated bodies? His own body was feeling heated now, for instance. And it didn't sound safe to move around with this stuff in the desert. No Old Spice for Jeddah, Mr Haq.

Why would an Italian, resident in Malta, hide a left-luggage receipt for twenty jumbo spray cans of shaving cream inside his wig? Because he stole it. The wop goes about looking like a total twat with his blow-dried ringlets, but they're just acting as a hiding place. He stole it, of course, and now I've got it. You steal my porn mags, I'll steal your left-luggage receipt. But what are twenty cans of shaving foam worth? Well, not $550, anyway. Unless . . .

Blum took off his shirt and then his boots too, his Spanish ankleboots. The sweat was running down him, in spite of the cold temperature of this small room with its man-made fibre carpet and plastic furniture, and the tarty pink lamp over the creaking single bed. He picked up a can, blew the wood-wool packing off it, and shook it. It weighed rather heavy in his hand, and something inside moved. Then he took off the white plastic cap and carefully pressed the dispenser. Hm. Not much pressure there. A little air, then a squiggle of white foam on his thumb. He smelled it. Again, no doubt: that was the "fresh, masculine fragrance of Old Spice" as promised on the can. Astringent whipped cream.

Blum went into the bathroom and sprayed another squiggle of shaving foam into the tub. Then the can uttered a sigh, and no more came out. Not a generous amount of foam for a 10-ounce can. Definitely a lot of wastage. But the can was still heavy. It must weigh half a pound, probably more. And all the others, he discovered, were equally heavy. Blum felt a tingling under his scalp. Keep out of this, my friend, a voice warned him, but it was not a particularly loud voice. It made little headway against the other voices he was hearing, and none at all against the tingling.

He sat down on the floor with the can and his penknife, and removed the plastic dispenser. Two cigarette lengths down in the can, he found a cellophane bag of white power and fished it out. Then he opened the cellophane bag, touched a damp finger to the powder, and tasted it.

10

"For someone who's spent a year in the Med you don't look good," said the man, who himself looked white as a sheet and did not move from his leather sofa.

"I haven't had much sleep recently," said Blum, stirring the sugar in his coffee cup. "And life everywhere is just as hectic as here."

"Right again. No one really needs to set foot out of the door these days."

Blum looked at the view. Old snow lay on the rooftops. The sky was like a dirty asphalt lid above them, and that was about all you could see from up in this penthouse. The northern parts of Munich were not a particularly attractive sight on a Sunday in March.

"Great view, right?"

"At least you've solved the suicide problem here, Hermes."

Hermes smiled and lit his Gauloise with a gold lighter. He was a thin man of about average height and uncertain age, and always wore black. The penthouse was sparsely furnished, but the sparse furnishings themselves were top quality, and they were drinking Jamaican coffee. A large pot stood on a hotplate. The girl on the double bed was top quality too, Eurasian and aged seventeen at the most. She was reading Camus, *L'Homme révolté*. Blum took an HB out of its crumpled packet and lit it with his disposable lighter.

"But you didn't crawl out of bed or some stand-up bar this fine day, and take a plane to Munich, just to discuss my suicide problems, am I right?"

Hermes's voice gave no clue to his origins. With his black hair combed back and his aquiline nose, he could have been Levantine, but Blum happened to know that he had come to Berlin in 1965 from a small town in Lower Saxony, and since then had been in the drugs trade without ever having trouble with the police. Maybe he had a couple of irons in the fire at this very moment. The Eurasian girl turned a page and chewed her thumbnail. Hermes gave an Oriental kind of smile.

"No," said Blum at last.

"Good," said Hermes, with that smile. "So what's it all about?"

"Cocaine," said Blum.

The Eurasian girl cast him a fleeting glance – the first since he had entered the penthouse – and ran her hand through the silky hair that fell to her knees. Hermes frowned.

"You want some cocaine from me?"

"No, I have some."

"Well, Blum, I must say you surprise me."

Hermes cautiously placed his feet in their black slippers on the carpet, as if to test the load-bearing properties of the floor, then stood up, threw his cigarette end into an alabaster container with a rubber plant reaching to the ceiling, and poured himself another cup of coffee.

Blum knew that Hermes was waiting for further explanations, but he had no intention of offering any. Finally Hermes smiled and went to the telephone, which stood on an Empire bureau. He dialled a number that he knew by heart, said a couple of words so quietly that Blum couldn't make them out, and hung up again. Then he bent down, chose a disc from the piles lying about on the carpet, and put it on the player without turning it on. The Eurasian girl turned another page. Either she had taken a course in speed reading or she knew the book by heart already, and was just picking out the best bits here and there. Or perhaps she was only pretending to read, and was recording the conversation with a wireless microphone fitted under her thumbnail . . .

"We'll discuss it later," said Hermes, when he was lying on the sofa again. "I'm no expert in that field, as you know."

"I know," said Blum, smiling back.

"And how was your trip, Blum? Did they treat you right? Was the food tolerable? Have you had new and fascinating experiences?"

"Can't complain," said Blum. "I never stayed anywhere for long."

"Ah, no, you're a pro. I've retired really, you know. I'm devoting myself to bringing up my daughter."

Blum saw the look Hermes gave the Eurasian girl.

"That's her?"

"What did you think, you old lecher? Thought I was taking children to bed?"

"It's a problem we all have some time or other," said Blum.

"Get yourself a daughter of your own and it'll soon pass off. But in a way you're right, of course. I wish I could say I can finally boast of a little perception and a touch of purification, but of course it's no such thing. You're around forty too, right?"

"Yes. I know what you mean."

"Indeed. I think we could do with a whisky at this point."

46

This time he stood up quickly, moving with agility, found a decanter and two glasses and poured the whisky. He drank standing up, looking at the girl who was allegedly his daughter.

She suddenly smiled at him, a smile that almost took Blum's breath away. Then she rolled over on her other side, turning her back to the men and burying herself in her book. Blum wouldn't have thought it possible for a jeans-clad bottom to be so seductive.

The doorbell rang. Hermes pressed the buzzer. A small, stout man with horn-rimmed glasses and an attaché case appeared and peeled off a rabbit-fur coat.

"My scientific assistant," said Hermes. "Henri, this is Blum. A traveller by trade. Well, Blum, now let's see what you've brought with you."

Blum took a small tube intended to hold tablets out of his trouser pocket and gave it to Henri, who put it on the tea-table and opened his portable chemistry laboratory.

"Come on, have another Scotch while he takes a look at your stuff," said Hermes, filling their glasses. Blum would rather have watched what Henri was doing, but that probably wouldn't have been etiquette. He took his glass and sipped. Sleet was falling outside now, and the city looked like its own cemetery. Flocks of crows fluttered over the Olympic stadium.

"I've settled down since my daughter joined me," said Hermes, "otherwise I wouldn't be here now. Her mother's entered politics, so I had to do something."

"Politics?"

"Yes, everything's gone haywire over there in Asia. That's another reason I'm retiring. We're going to Switzerland next week to find her a boarding school. In Switzerland she'll make friends with the sons of the people her mother's fighting. Maybe I'll find myself a retirement home at the same time. Zurich wouldn't be a bad idea. Or maybe Lucerne?"

"So it's just coincidence I found you here?"

"My dear Blum, in this business one should never count on coincidence."

Henri cleared his laboratory away and handed Hermes the tube. Blum sipped his whisky again. His throat was dry. He saw that the Eurasian girl had disappeared.

"Peruvian flake," said Henri, "direct from the producer. Hasn't been cut yet. Ninety-eight per cent. The real McCoy."

"Flake? What does that mean?"

"It all depends on the refinement process," explained Henri. "As you may know, cocaine is made of coca paste, which in its own turn is made from the original substance, coca leaves. Normally the refinement process gives you cocaine powder, which is about 80–86 per cent pure cocaine. But if you refine the coca paste so that it dries into separate crystals you get what we call flakes. And they can be around 96 per cent pure. Pharmaceutical cocaine, for instance, is always 99 per cent strength and always comes in flakes. Take a look."

He tipped a flake on a small mirror and handed Blum his magnifying glass. Sure enough, Blum saw crystals glittering in the powder, like ice cubes in snow.

"But how do you know it comes from Peru?"

Henri shrugged and put his magnifying glass away. "Well, in time you get to know these things. There are only three possibilities – Colombia, Bolivia, Peru. Some of my colleagues claim that Bolivian cocaine is the strongest, but of course that's nonsense. It always depends on the refinement process. You have to learn about it, see? Learning on the spot is best, of course."

"Then let's see if we like it," said Hermes. For the first time he seemed to be the man Blum remembered. He took a small ivory case from the desk, pushed two straight lines of the cocaine into place on the mirror with a razor blade, and inhaled the cocaine through a rolled-up dollar bill. Then he breathed in deeply and passed the equipment over to Blum.

"These days they often cut it with the most extraordinary things – Italian baby laxative is about the most harmless. What's it called, Henri?"

"Mannite. Looks the same as coke under the magnifying glass, tastes the same, dissolves the same. They've taken to using yoghurt cultures too recently."

"Good heavens." Hermes lit a cigarette and drew on it deeply and with enjoyment. "Ah, really good stuff, Blum. Congratulations."

Congratulations for what, Blum would have liked to ask. Instead he handed the mirror on to Henri, who looked at him inquiringly. Blum shook his head.

"I don't feel like it."

"Have you ever done a line?" asked Hermes.

"Last year in Paris," said Blum. "It makes me too nervous."

"*Chacun à son goût*, that's all I can say."

Henri sniffed and then poured himself a whisky. His hands shook slightly.

"Did you bring this stuff into the country?" he asked Blum.

"Like I told you, Blum's a traveller by trade," said Hermes. "You pick up the oddest things abroad. Sometimes you even find something memorable. I think I want some music now." He lay back on the sofa, glass within reach, picked up something that looked like a TV remote control and pressed a button. The record player switched on. Henri sat down and leafed through a magazine. The only one of them not relaxing was Blum, who clutched his glass and stared at the bed.

"Charlie Parker," said Hermes, closing his eyes. "Charlie Parker All Star Sextet. Charlie Parker, alto; Miles Davis, trumpet; J. J. Johnson, trombone; Max Roach, drums; Duke Jordan, piano; Tommy Potter, bass."

But the music did not soothe Blum. Far from it – as usual with the music of Parker every note, however lightly, almost fleetingly played, seemed to set off a dark, painful echo. How people could listen to this for pleasure was a mystery to him. It was music with more shadows than Blum wanted to see just now, asking questions more difficult than he wanted to hear. Charlie Parker with "Out of Nowhere" on an afternoon in the north, with the sleet like a grey wall between the pent-house and the nearby motorway access road and supermarket centres, like a wall with Miles Davis blowing holes in it, but there was another wall behind it, said Charlie Parker, and yet another wall behind that. Don't let them get you down, thought Blum. This is your biggest chance in years, and you are damn well going to exploit it, and neither Charlie Parker nor the sleet nor Hermes with his drop-out blues is going to muck it up for you. What does drop-out blues mean anyway? That man never dropped out of anything. He'll just keep dropping in all the way to his funeral. You mustn't take your eye off the ball for a split second.

"Amazing," said Hermes, when the disc came to an end. "He has a shadow for every light and a question for every answer. Right, what sort of questions do we have now, Blum?"

"Do you know any buyers, Hermes?"

Hermes was standing at the window with his whisky.

"Listen, Blum, I'm not delivering a seminar, but here's a few essentials. The cocaine trade is something of a closed shop, and it's better for all concerned if it stays that way. We all know our own contacts, and that's it. So far there've only been people with clear heads in our line, and the customers show their appreciation with good money. Cocaine isn't a dirty affair like heroin. Perhaps it will be if it really becomes big business – in ten years, snorting coke probably *will* be big business, but for now we're still an exclusive circle. The advantage of that is that the cops can concentrate on their beloved heroin and the poor little pushers in the nearest U-Bahn toilets. That way it's easier for them to meet their quota of arrests too. Of course I know buyers, Blum – here comes the answer to your question – but I'm keeping them to myself until I'm right out of the trade. However, you'll have no difficulty getting rid of the few flakes you've got there; I'll buy them from you. Even I don't get my hands on such good snow so often. How much of it do you have?"

Blum was prepared for this question. Not for nothing had he lain awake all night, watching the factory chimneys and garbage incinerators emerging from the morning twilight. He mustn't tell anyone just how much he had.

"Here."

He put the small cellophane bag he had filled with cocaine that morning on the tea-table. About one-tenth of the contents of a can. Henri weighed the bag on a light metal precision scale with mother-of-pearl ornamentation.

"Exactly 11.35 grams."

"Excellent," said Hermes. "I can survive Switzerland better with that. You're sure you don't have any more?"

He gave his Oriental smile. Blum smiled back.

"I wouldn't sell even this if I wasn't nearly broke."

"Right, I'll give you a cheque."

"Maybe we should agree the price first," said Blum.

"Just as you like. What's the price per gram at the moment, Henri?"

"Two hundred marks for the usual stuff, cut. For flakes, uncut, you could ask around 300."

"You wouldn't get it, though. But that's not the way I operate, and Blum needs the money. So let's say for 11.35 – given the usual discount between friends – well, I'll give you a cheque for 2,400 marks."

"I'm only accepting cash, Hermes."

This seemed to displease Hermes.

"Cash?" He uttered that delightful word as if it were the punchline of a joke in poor taste told in a bar. "Oh, come on, Blum, cash on a Sunday? I never keep money in the house, understand? I only ever pay by credit card. Do you have any cash, Henri?"

"Cash?" Henri made it sound like a slightly dirtier version of the joke. He searched his pockets, a derisive smile on his lips. "A tenner – but I need that myself to fill up the car."

"I thought everyone dealt in cash in your line," said Blum.

"Usually, Blum. Not always. And when they do it's shifted at once, laundered, stashed away in investments."

Blum took back the bag.

"Then it's no deal," he said, making as if to go.

"Oh, come along," said Hermes, "hold on a minute. Sit down in this nice chair and have another nice whisky and enjoy the nice view and give me an hour or so, and then you can have it in cash."

Hermes left. Blum lit an HB, his last. He really needed that cash. Numbers clicked through his head like the coloured figures in the fruit machines: 10×12 $= 120 \ldots 120 \times 20 = 2{,}400 \ldots 2{,}400 \times 200 = 480{,}000 \ldots$ Bingo. Henri leafed through his magazine, and when he had finished it he picked up another. He didn't deign to address another word to Blum. Perhaps someone with a mere 11.35 grams was beneath Henri's notice, even if it was Peruvian flake, 96 per cent. Blum fed the number 300 into his calculations instead of 200. That would make 720,000. Better stick with 200, he told himself. Let's not go mad. He stared out at the sleet. In the dim light, the coloured figures shot up and down in his head.

It was over two hours before Hermes was back with the DM 2,400. He took the bag of coke and gave Blum the money.

"That right?"

Blum held his gaze. "That's okay, Hermes."

Then Hermes took a pinch of the bluish snow, and his daughter came into the room. She was now wearing a long, peach-coloured silk housecoat, and she set out tea things. The look she gave Blum, however, had nothing inviting about it.

"You'll stay to tea, will you, Blum?" asked Hermes.

"A cup of tea wouldn't hurt."

When he left Parker and Dizzy Gillespie were playing "Perdido". Henri was snorting a line. Hermes was lying on the sofa, and the Eurasian girl was sitting beside him, holding his hand and reading *L'Homme révolté*.

Outside, the slush trickled over the top of his ankleboots at every step he took. The supermarket on the corner had a placard advertising its offer of the week. "GOOD THINGS COME IN SMALL CANS", said the ad.

11

That evening Blum went to a party. A girl with her hair dyed green, and a freckled nose on the end of which he saw a trace of cocaine, had given him the address in a café on Leopoldstrasse, where he was sitting thinking about his next move. The girl was in the company of two unisex figures with safety-pins in their ears, and seemed to be inviting anyone who looked a likely prospect to this party. Perhaps she saw Blum as a classic example of the bourgeois type. That was okay by him – good camouflage was extremely important now. And he had long considered himself a classic.

The villa belonged to a writer and stood in a garden run wild. A rowing boat was rotting away among the bushes. Crows on the garage roof, a half-moon on the skyline, the house brightly illuminated, garlands of lights even in the garden, where sleet was still falling, and in all the rooms loud music, a crush of people, confused voices.

"We're moving to the country," his hostess told him. "The mortgage rates here are sending us just crazy. My husband will be able to work again in the country, and I shall grow vegetables. Do you write too?"

"Only figures," said Blum. The hostess in her model dress was already moving on to greet the next guests. Blum helped himself to whisky. This writer didn't seem to be doing so badly. The tables in the big room were groaning under the weight of dishes: soups and salads, platters of hors d'œuvres, champagne buckets, shining batteries of bottles of wine and whisky. Blum helped himself to a seafood salad, following it up with a powerful chilli dish and some cheese. He watched the guests. Although most of them were his age, they wore an air of carefree youth. Many of the women seemed to be in hysterical high spirits. The few really young people, on the other hand, despite their bizarre appearance, bore themselves like accountants unable to conceal their glances of disapproval, even after working hours. Blum soon felt slightly nostalgic for Larry's nightmares, Mr Haq's fantasies, those Thursday evenings in the Pegasus Bar. He put his plate down and went to look round the house.

The old guard of pot-heads were assembled in a darkened room. Candles, musky scents, Afro hairstyles, lilac dungarees, loads of Indian jewellery, a nargileh in the middle of the room and the inevitable idiot fidgeting with bongo drums by the wall. Blum took the little tube of snow out of his pocket. They were interested.

"A gram costs—"

"Oh, come on, man, cool it!"

The fact that Blum insisted on cash payment defused suspicion but made him appear rapacious. He put the tube away again.

"Sorry, friends, all you get on credit is the Vienna Woods."

"Vienna Woods yourself," said the girl with green hair.

"Bad karma, that," said one man dressed Indian-style. The Stones were wailing from all the loudspeakers:

> "Please, Cousin Cocaine, place
> your cool hands on my head
> Hey, Sister Morphine, you better
> make up my bed . . ."

Blum wandered into the next room. A flickering candle on the windowsill, two chess players in thoughtful mood in front of a board. Nothing to be got out of them for sure. They already had their kicks. On the first floor, a beauty with a Madonna face was putting up with the conversation of two useless characters.

"He's finished, I tell you, absolutely finished, a burnt-out case, done for – all he does is repeat himself . . ."

"But he started brilliantly, you have to admit. That half-dead woman with the Nazi boots photographed through the striptease ad, no one's going to trump that in a hurry . . ."

The Madonna nodded devoutly.

A balding, four-square man in a dinner jacket approached Blum. "I just heard there's charlie in the house. Is that you?"

"Sorry, my name's Blum."

"No, no, man, I mean charlie like C, like in coke, get it? Is that you?"

And here came the creative characters, the opinion-formers, clad in their 50 per cent silk mix: the creators of films, books, art, fashion, newspapers, able to soften you up, to chat you up. They all seemed very stylish, but when Blum mentioned cash they couldn't produce the goods: "Not in funds at the moment, old boy, but call me in a couple of weeks, then I'll have the new advertising budget . . . my production expenses . . . the money from Bonn . . . my legacy from Hamburg . . . my wife's salary . . . the money from the Goethe Institute . . . the dough from the Intelligence Agency . . ."

"The Federal Intelligence Agency?"

"Even Intelligence is getting into cultural politics, and about time too, I may say. When I think what the CIA's wasted its money on . . ."

"Who said anything about cultural policy? I'm talking about a pound of cocaine."

"My good friend, haven't you ever heard of the opium aura?"

Blum understood. Life was hard but art was even harder, you couldn't twist a person's arm. But Blum, unfortunately, had to twist their arms.

"I really do need cash, friends. Maybe you could try getting a little credit?"

But they probably wouldn't believe I have five pounds of coke under my bed in the Metropol, he thought as he walked on. They can probably tell that I haven't yet got beyond trying a few assorted jobs – a freight-car of European Community butter, a Titian, a load of Danish porn mags. You lot have Bonn behind you, or Federal Intelligence, or at least culture. I have to take what comes. And when it comes I have to try to sell it as dear as possible.

He went on looking around. All the guests were making the most of their chances. A poet was sitting under a blue lamp holding court. He was drinking wine from a two-litre bottle and playing a note on a jew's harp now and then. His audience was fascinated.

"He's overcome the symptoms of his block – complete recovery is close," said a gay man, repeating it into the cassette recorder someone brought him.

"Got a cigarette on you, mate?"

A man with the beard of an old seadog and the eyes of a basset hound brought up in an animal shelter tapped Blum with a nicotine-stained finger. They drank a whisky together.

"I've published six volumes of poetry – two of them with famous firms – and I've written twenty-one radio plays and a hundred essays on the spirit of the times," confessed the seadog, "but one day suddenly none of it was worth anything – we don't need any more arts sections, they said in the editorial offices, we want the raw originality of the production line, the cogwheels of psychic impoverishment. All demolished overnight, over and done with – as if I wasn't being ground down by those cogwheels myself. Is that bottle empty? If you don't know where to spend the night there's still a corner free in Prince Gorki's potato cellar . . ."

Shortly after midnight Blum noticed some of the scroungers filling their coat pockets with leftovers from the cold buffet. *I could use a man like you, Mr Blum.* Oh, children, children. He left his corner and went on exploring the house. If he couldn't find any buyers he might at least look for a woman.

A shaven-headed character in a shimmering silk shirt was now squatting in the room where the two men had been playing chess, a snake around his neck. Three incense candles were burning, and in the sultry haze above a mattress three sari-clad women were holding hands and uttering throaty sounds at rhythmic intervals, with their eyes closed:

"Awawawa – ah!"

"Ululululu – uh!"

A film projector was whirring in a large, darkened room. The film was black and white and taken without artificial lighting, but the images left no doubt about the action: a woman was being torn apart by three bloodhounds while a naked man masturbated. The audience did not seem happy with the film.

"Aesthetically it leaves much to be desired," explained a man with a Wagnerian quiff of hair. "You don't show people suffering unless art permeates every moment of that suffering as the immanent will towards an aesthetic."

In the kitchen a man in a cardigan and brogues was eating pea soup, and the hostess of the party – now wearing a severely cut riding outfit – was saying, "I do hope you're all having a good time. My husband hopes so too, don't you, darling?"

"No," said the man in the cardigan, fishing a piece of pork out of his soup. "I hate the cinema, I hate art. Joseph Goebbels was 100 per cent right: when he heard the word culture, he reached for his gun. Unfortunately I don't have one or I'd mow you all down."

"The critics misunderstood his last novel so badly," explained the writer's wife.

"They understood it perfectly well," said the man, with his mouth full. A pea rolled down his chin.

Blum found himself beside a small, slim woman with long, dark hair who was gazing sadly at the writer. She wore a long dress that emphasized her slender figure. Blum pressed a glass of champagne into her hand, which had a wedding ring on it. She took the glass and smiled at him, surprised.

"Come along," said Blum, "and I'll show you something."

They went out into the hall and found a place to sit beside a lesbian couple.

"He was once so gifted," said the woman, "and now all this wretched stuff. Why do they go to the bad so quickly, can you tell me?"

She looked at Blum as if his answer really interested her. Blum nodded, like a man who asks himself such questions on a daily basis.

"One never tires of talent. He delivered the goods by the yard, made a killing and then gorged on it."

"You say that very certainly."

"Something wrong with it?"

"No, probably not. What about you?"

"Oh, I'm in another line entirely."

He produced the tube and opened it. He had not been wrong. She knew what it was and took a pinch at once.

"That's great," she said. "So are you the character who has so much of it and is selling for cash only?"

"Was your husband one of those men in dinner jackets?"

"My husband's in a monastery in Thailand."

"Good heavens, what's he doing there?"

"I imagine he's looking for himself. Perhaps he's looking for me too. Or for a cure for hay fever. You know, you're not at all the type to be dealing in cocaine."

"Is there a definite type?"

She laughed, and put a hand on his arm.

12

"Like some more snow?"

"No thanks, I only ever take a very little. To the Incas, coca was a gift of the gods, and now we've made cocaine of it. A business."

"Well, we can't be expected to turn into Incas."

"That's why I try to see more in the powder than just an expensive pleasure. What about you? Don't you use it at all?"

"Yes, but even less often than you. And not at all while I'm dealing in it."

"Do you think you'll succeed?"

"Why not?"

"Drugs aren't like vegetables, Blum. They're magic. They're connected to force-fields beyond our control."

"Tell that to the Mafia. They'll fall about laughing."

"But you're not the Mafia. I don't want to discourage you, far from it – I think it'd be fantastic if you can bring it off. But you have to adjust to the magic, or the stuff will destroy you. It's more powerful than any of the people who sell it."

"Mm. So this character in Frankfurt is a friend of yours?"

"For heaven's sake, no. All I know is that he's quite big in the trade."

"How big?"

"Like I said, quite big. Just how big you may find out. I'll call him tomorrow morning and make you an appointment."

"He's someone you have to make an appointment with?"

"Believe me, it's best. Then you can call him at the number I'll give you now."

He had her write the number on the back of Hackensack's business card.

"That's really nice of you. What's your name?"

"I need a glass of champagne now."

She did not come back. He didn't even know her name. The brunette: that would have to do. Hermes was right, some things were memorable, and as a rule they weren't great fucks or the sound of Niagara Falls, but fleeting moments, twilights, dark eyes, the ball settling on number 17 after all.

He went into the garden. By now real snow was falling again. The flakes hovered down to settle on the garlands and melted on the brightly coloured lights. The trees were black with crows. Party guests were strolling about underneath them. Many were unsteady on their legs, and some of them fell over. You'd have to be a masochist or pissed as a newt to get any fun out of dancing on the gravel drive, which was now full of cars, and on the slushy lawn under the scornful eyes of the punks and to their damnably simple music. The drunks danced in the dirt, the punks threw shards of broken champagne bottles and snowballs containing gravel at them, and the crows sat on the rooftops and in the trees waiting – tourists of darkness.

Blum was going indoors again when two men barred his way. One was grey-haired and wore a white suit, the other was younger and clad in leather garments of some kind.

"You the one with the nose candy?" asked the elder man.

"You mean me?"

"Of course he is. See that blazer?" said the younger man, who had moved rather close to Blum. "Bring it out, will you? We fancy some."

Not cops, then, private initiative. Blum shifted his weight to his other foot.

"If you're in funds, sure."

"Let's have a look," said the elder man, who did not seem quite to have made up his mind whether to join in.

"Come on, bring it out."

"Well, I can show you . . ."

Blum made as if to put his hand in his jacket pocket, and as the younger man watched his movement he kicked the toe of his boot into the man's soft parts as hard as he could and grabbed the older man's arm. The man tore himself away and kicked out at Blum, but made contact only with a plaster statue. It fell to the ground. Blum jumped off the steps and forced his way through the dancing guests and out into the street. The punks were bellowing. He looked around. The two men were following him. A woman in a fur coat was just unlocking the door of a sports car.

"It's the cops!" shouted Blum. "Take me with you!"

She got into the car, and for a moment he thought she was going to drive away without him, but then she opened the passenger door and waved him in. As he closed the door she drove off. Blum did not look round. Perhaps it had all been just his imagination and they meant to be friendly. Some people don't express themselves well, everyone knows that. At least he was sitting beside a woman again. In a sports car this time. The cocaine trade wasn't getting off to a bad start.

"Thanks very much," said Blum. "Do you by any chance have a cigarette too?"

She tapped the glove compartment casually. Blum took out an open Reyno packet and lit one. The woman had short black hair, a hooked nose, a brightly painted mouth and a long neck. She was wearing a man's pin-stripe suit. He guessed that she was in her mid-forties; the veins on the backs of her hands stood out. He had seen her before – beside the man with the passion for Wagner who had not been convinced by the aesthetics of the horror porn film.

"I know who you are," said the woman, looking at him with a smile.

"Then perhaps you'd rather drop me off round the next corner."

"On the contrary – I'm taking you straight back to my place."

"You haven't fallen desperately in love with me, have you?"

"Love – that's a dirty word! I was thinking of the cocaine you're selling."

"But the cops are after me."

Now she was smiling as hyenas might smile on seeing a dying victim suddenly pick himself up.

"That was only my husband and his gay friend. They didn't hurt you, did they?"

"I got the impression that was what they had in mind."

"They're making heavy weather of it. Physical inten-sity and all that. They were really just supposed to bring you my way."

"They succeeded, then."

Things were getting rather too hot for Blum. He hadn't imagined the cocaine trade quite like this. The sooner he got rid of the stuff the better.

"Seeing you don't want to seduce me I guess you want to abduct me. That was a red light, by the way."

"With a radar device fitted, yes. But I'm in a hurry. Are you frightened?"

"I wouldn't be dealing in coke if I was."

"I find fear so erotic. But I'm not abducting you either. I just want your coke."

"You could have done it more easily. Like I was just telling your husband, so long as you're in funds . . ."

She turned into a side street, almost taking a pedestrian with her.

"Oh, but a little drama's all part of it, Mr Blum."

"How do you know my name?"

"Munich's like a village. I'm Renée."

She held out her hand as if expecting a kiss. Blum stubbed out the Reyno. He'd never liked those menthol things. He'd had enough of the woman and enough of Munich. She withdrew her hand and parked the car in front of an entrance. This was a rather dark area, full of old-fashioned buildings.

"Thanks for the lift, but this is where our ways part," said Blum, reaching for the door handle. "So much drama is bad for my heart."

"No, no, my dear Herr Blum, you can't go now. Everything's ready."

Blum got out and slammed the car door. Two figures emerged from the shadows and stepped into the light of the street lamps. Of course, the husband and his friend. Perhaps they'd hitched a ride on a helicopter.

"Well, boys, fancy a second round?"

"This is not a very nice guy you've picked, Renée," said her husband sadly.

The woman took Blum's arm.

"Now, let's all go upstairs without any fuss and make friends. And then . . ."

"I think you're all rather overestimating yourselves," said Blum, breaking free and running for it. He was in luck – the road was gritted here. He had reached the corner when Renée shouted, "You'll pay for this, Blum!"

Her voice was like the voice of a brewer's drayman who was going to be a jackal in his next life.

But I won't pay you, thought Blum, hailing a taxi. Sighing, he leaned back on the upholstery and mopped the sweat from his brow. It was still winter here, but you got to sweat more than in the south. The bar in the Metropol was still open, but although as he reached reception he could hear the voice of the drunk whose husband gave introductory seminars on stocks and shares to the inmates of Stadelheim, Blum went into it, taking his key. He urgently needed something as normal as beer.

This time she was not alone at the bar, but she was still the only woman, and it didn't seem to be doing her any good. She was clutching a man's suit with her left hand and a brandy glass with her right and trying to play the vamp. Her trouser suit was stained. Ash had left grey streaks on its yellow fabric, and she had spilled red wine on it too. The red-faced men sitting around her on bar stools looked as if they were waiting for her to fall over and open her legs. Beer, sweat and Chanel No. 5. The Arabs were sitting in the corner again, staring at the drunks. They've made sure of a front seat for the gang rape, thought Blum, trying to order a beer as unobtrusively as possible. But the Yugoslav ignored him. Then the blonde spotted him.

"There you are, you faithless man!" The men smirked. "But you've had something better than liana wine today, right? He drank nothing but liana wine for three whole years, you know, when he was with the Hottentots."

"Just what it looks like," Blum heard someone say.

The Yugoslav put a cognac down in front of him. Blum shook his head.

"From the lady," said the Yugoslav.

"He can't take it any more," suggested one of the men. The blood rose to Blum's head, but he said nothing. With five pounds of cocaine under your bed, you don't start brawling with drunks.

"I'll have a beer," he said, emptying the cognac at a single gulp. It was Mariacron. The Yugoslav must have conceived a healthy dislike of him. Blum smiled at the blonde over his empty glass. Yesterday he had almost got into bed with her; today he just felt sorry for her. One of the men already had his paw on her behind. The Arabs ordered more coffee. They did not seem to care about the hostile looks of the sales reps, for whom every rise in the price of fuel was a blow below the belt. Perhaps they actually owned the hotel.

Blum got his beer, and as he drank it he felt the eyes of the blonde on him and tried not to hear what she was saying in her befuddled state, until suddenly he did hear it, indeed he heard it very clearly, because she was talking about him.

"—and then the porter put down this carton full of shaving foam – shaving foam, I ask you! And he was talking so big about the Amazon." She saw that he was listening and turned directly to him. "Am I right or am I right? Well, if you have all that shaving foam you could at least shave properly."

This set the reps roaring with laughter. Spluttering, whinnying laughter, with much thigh-slapping, and the man with the big paw was now openly kneading her bottom. Blum stayed calm. But the drunks were now moving in on him.

"You're standing on my foot, mate."

"Oh, am I?" The man had a face like runny Camembert sprinkled with paprika, and his eyes were focusing with difficulty. "Didn't you hear? You want to shave properly!"

Blum slowly withdrew his foot from under the other man's. If the Camembert toppled over now there would be a brawl. He put several coins on the bar and tried to get away.

"Talks big but can't hold his beer any more," said the man with the paw that was now slipping up the blonde's back. Suddenly she rose from her swivel stool – the back of it promptly knocked the beer glass out of her suitor's hand – and let herself fall past him and to the floor, burying the glass under her. The men went on talking as if nothing had happened, except for her suitor, who was complaining about his beer. Blum helped the woman up again. Tears were running down her face, dissolving her makeup. The smell of cognac and perfume was overpowering.

"Terribly sorry," she stammered, "only looking for my husband. Where can the man be?"

"Here's some men for you," boomed someone.

"I wish I knew why anyone would want so much shaving foam," wondered the man with the Camembert face.

"Ask him then, Otto."

"Hey, you, what do you want with a whole carton full of shaving foam?"

He bellowed so loud that you could hear him all over the lobby. The Arabs looked expectantly at Blum.

"I'm sure he'll be here soon," Blum told the blonde, propping her against the bar. Her smeared, swollen face smiled happily at him.

"He sells the foam to those Hottentots!" bellowed the man with the big paw.

"And we pay the subsidy!"

This gleaned general approval. The Hottentots really needed that foam.

"You're so cute," said the blonde, fluttering her clogged lashes. "Come on, let's have another."

But Blum disengaged himself and left, yet again – for the third time in three days – with a woman shouting after him. It was beginning to get him down. Then he heard her fall full length once more. This time she stayed down, shrieking like a stuck pig. When he reached the lift he saw the night porters hurrying into the bar.

"Disgusting," said a blue-rinsed American woman just coming in from seeing the night life of Munich.

"It's only a movie," said Blum, putting his sunglasses on. The American got straight out of the lift again.

When he was back in room 316 Blum took a deep breath. This is getting tougher than you expected, he thought. It's all the extra fuss makes the thing so tricky. He stared at a notice on the wall: FOR YOUR SAFETY. It told him what to do in case of a fire in the hotel. The last sentence ran: "Keep calm – do not panic – thank you!" Right, thought Blum. I hope I can bear that in mind.

It was a long time before he could get to sleep. He leafed through the Bahamas handbook. One Mr Bernard Butler, a resident there for ten years, said of Freetown, the new city on Grand Bahama, "Everything is just the way we like it here," and perhaps you didn't need to work for the Mafia to get a piece of the cake there, raisins and all – but wasn't Blum already working for the Mafia? It was part of the game, and you couldn't count on chance. He switched off the light and looked out at the tower. A red eye blinked on top of it, registering everything. No one's going to give you a chance, thought Blum. Maybe that's just what will bring you through. I'm an amateur in the cocaine trade, but I've had forty years' experience of survival.

He fiddled with his transistor radio and picked up a woman's voice on short wave, broadcasting coded news to people who were experts in their field, and at last the endless columns of numbers of her code, as well as that dream of the white beaches, began to make him drowsy . . .

"14811 – 34210 – 42734 – 38307 – 15759 – 61003 – 21536 – 89342" – palms, a gentle breeze, a sunrise sky – "99188 – 50777 – 53338 – 73512 – 39834 – 93631 – 47345" – "this stuff is more powerful than any of the people who sell it" – "51120 – 43943 – 37518 – 65343" – "I could use a man like you," said a hyena, snapping at his throat. He woke up bathed in sweat. Dawn was slowly crawling over the rooftops and the red eye went out. But he knew the controllers were everywhere, checking up on him.

13

Monday, mid-day, bright sun, little Bavarian clouds, a blue and white sky. Blum bought a used sample case from a Turk, artificial leather, black, 21 × 14 inches, DM 85.

"Anything else, sir?"

"Do you have a good knife?"

The man smiled broadly and showed his collection. Blum chose one with a mother-of-pearl handle, 9 inches long, made in Solingen, sharp as a razor blade. The man oiled the flick mechanism.

"That way you're one tenth of a second faster, friend."

In his hotel room, Blum packed the cans into the case. It neatly took twenty, and indeed would have taken twenty-one, but he wasn't greedy. He stowed one tablet tube full of the powder and the can it came from in his trouser pockets. You had to have something at the ready. At the reception desk he asked about the blonde. The clerk acted as if he knew nothing about her. A busload of Swedish women surged through the revolving doors into the hotel. Blondes, drunk; they came cheaper by the dozen. They were not to Blum's taste. He left no tip.

Another light beer in the rail station buffet, the sample case on a chair beside him. Around here Munich was still the capital of junk-shops and cattle dealers, North Africans and Hopfperle beer. Bullnecked men from the Allgäu, looking over the top of the *Memminger Boten* newspaper, watched the Macedonian pickpockets miming intimate relations with the big-bosomed wait-resses, and itinerant quack doctors from Bohemia were recruiting assistants from among the unemployed sons of the Anatolian garbage men. The finishing touch was put to Blum's mid-day contentment by the appearance of the Salvation Army. Six plump-cheeked girls sang, "Hallelujah, God be with you", and a martial gentle-man who must hold the rank of field marshal at least distributed a tract from which Blum learned that Bob Dylan the protest singer had been born again. It seemed a suitable conclusion to the 1970s, just as the cocaine in Blum's sample case promised a good begin-ning to the 1980s. Blum rewarded the Salvation Army with a five-mark piece and went to catch his Intercity 624, departing 13.16 hours (Würzburg – Frankfurt am Main – Cologne – Wuppertal – Dortmund).

Of course they could be anywhere, he thought, look-ing at the man in the blue maxi-coat standing by the sausage stall and immersed in the *Corriere della Sera* – Rossi, or the people he had pinched the stuff from or meant to pinch it from, or friend Hermes, Madame Renée, and of course the police, the Federal German CID, the Federal Intelligence Agency, Interpol, the CIA, how's things, Mr Hackensack – and that's just what they'll assume, they'll assume you're going to crack up, give in, surrender, take the coke back to counter 1 at the left-luggage office for safekeeping and send the receipt to the Phoenicia. Paranoia, that's the word. Persecution mania. Those pangs at the heart, this ache in the kidneys, the tingling up your back-bone, the itch under your scalp, all just persecution mania. Keep cool. You've made up your mind to see this thing through, so do that, go to the dining car with the depressed look of a traveller in thermal underwear, no business deal done all last week, these chemicals will finish us off, the wife's got the curse, Hertha Football Club has lost again, and a long week in Wuppertal is staring you in your beer-fuddled face.

"A Pils, waiter, nice and cold."

That was the right kind of tone. Now just a little more distaste in the voice.

"And a Pichelsteiner stew, that's about all that's worth eating in this dump."

"Just what I always say," commented a man, sitting down with Blum, although there were several empty tables. Blum pressed his legs against the sample case under the seat and looked at his travelling companion. Roundish face, neat parting, steel-rimmed glasses, grey suit, tie and waistcoat. Could be about thirty-five, but one of those faces that never age, they just die some time or other. He placed a large book in a brown paper cover beside his cutlery and put a Lord Extra in his mouth.

"Do you travel by train often?" asked Blum.

The man nodded deliberately. Perhaps a little too much the stolid citizen to be a possible member of Rossi's syndicate. Looked more like a cop. Which meant he probably was in the syndicate after all. Blum felt himself breaking out in a sweat. And the train had only reached the suburb of Pasing.

"Far too often," said the man, "but it's all in the day's work, so you have to accept it."

The steward brought Blum an ice-cold Pils. At least he'd hit the right note with the man. His neighbour at table ordered an Apollinaris and a Mozart Toast, a fillet steak dish.

"But not well done, medium rare," he said almost pleadingly. The steward muttered something and moved away. "Doesn't taste so good well done," added the man, as if he had to justify himself.

"Why not have the Pichelsteiner?"

"I had a Pichelsteiner only on Friday," said the man, opening his book. Not until they had eaten – the Mozart Toast was overdone, of course, and the Pichelsteiner delicious – did they fall into conversation again. Blum would have talked to anyone, even a deaf mute. Anything was better than constantly looking at the door through which a man with a machine gun might appear any moment – but that was just in the movies. In real life the syndicate was sitting there at the table, pushing away his plate with the remains of the steak. He took a Lord Extra out of its packet and said, "I wonder if you'd mind doing me a favour."

Here we go, thought Blum.

"It's like this, you see – I didn't quite meet my quota yesterday evening."

What was all this? The confessions of an overworked killer? The man lit his cigarette and rubbed his thumb over the spine of the book. "Reptiles. I had a pet slow-worm as a boy, maybe that's what made me think of it as a subject."

Blum relaxed. At the worst this character might be with Intelligence. He was quite red in the face now.

"Do you have an exam ahead?"

"No, no, I'm a vacuum cleaner engineer. But these days I specialize in quiz shows. Repairing vacuum cleaners all your life – well, that's kind of monotonous. Haven't you seen me on TV?"

"I get to see relatively little TV," said Blum. "What do you do on television?"

"Oh, I appear on quiz shows. Maybe you've seen me after all – I mean, people don't always watch very closely. *The After Nine Quiz Show, Who's the Brainbox?, The Big Question?* No? We get high ratings, though. I made my debut in *Movie Buffs.* But you can only win the top prize on a show once, so if you're a pro you have to be versatile."

Blum agreed. He leaned back. "Do you do it full time?"

"What's the alternative? Learning by heart is a full-time job. Of course my good memory comes in useful. History was my strong point at school – I could remember all the dates. Try me out – ask me a question!"

"What about?"

"A historical event!"

"What kind of historical event?"

"Oh, come on, you must know a historical event!"

The man was getting annoyed. The classic agent type, decided Blum. Didn't seem to be interested in coke, but mad keen on the past.

"Or just tell me your phone number and I'll tell you what happened in the year matching it. That's it, give me your phone number!"

Hm. Only a beginner could be that obvious. "Okay. 44 34 59."

The man leaned back, frowning. "That's really your phone number? Rather a tricky one."

"I thought you said you could come up with a historical event for *any* set of figures."

"I can. Right, here we go: forty-four, of course, we have 44 BC, assassination of Caesar. Thirty-four ... that's trickier. Oh, I know: the murder of Wallenstein, 1634. And fifty-nine, let's say 1759, battle of Kunersdorf."

"Oh yes? And what happened then?"

"What do you mean, what happened?"

"In this battle – what was it about?"

"Oh, that's not interesting. But you do see I can't go on repairing vacuum cleaners, not with a memory like that, can I?"

"Yes, I see. So now?"

"I need to go over the crocodiles again. Page 128."

The large tome was Volume 6 of Grzimek's *Animal Encyclopedia*. Blum opened it. A crocodile blinked out at him. Not really, of course, but that was what it looked like. The crocodile was lying in the sun by a river, its jaws were wide open, and it seemed to be very much at ease.

"Go on, then," said Blum, lighting an HB.

"The crocodile is a member of the subclass of large saurians. We distinguish between three families that are still extant, the alligator family, the true crocodile family, and the gavial family. Among alligators, we distinguish between the alligator genus, the spectacled caiman genus . . ."

The man had learned his quota all right. Blum wondered what this farce was in aid of. Of course, human life would be intolerable without such fooling around. Crocodiles had lived on earth 18 million years longer than mankind, and there was a pretty good chance they would still be around when humanity's fooling around had finished it off.

By the time they reached Würzburg they were through with the work quota. The quiz expert rewarded himself with a third Apollinaris, and Blum ordered his seventh Pils. The pressure on his bladder was frightful, but he didn't move from the spot. This man was capable of anything.

"So how long have you been doing quizzes?"

"Almost four years. Of course it takes a while before you feel happy on TV. Stage fright, you know. I can tell you, when there's 20 million people out there waiting for you to have no idea of the date of the battle of Aboukir, or the name of the film where Marlon Brando played a Japanese, or the number of genuses of pythons in existence – well, you may be good, but you suddenly get the feeling you're sitting in the middle of space with nothing underneath you, know what I mean?"

"I'm not unfamiliar with the feeling," said Blum.

"And what's your line, if I may ask?"

"I'm in the construction industry."

"Ah, well, of course that's quite something. With the economic fluctuations . . ."

"You can say that again. And again," said Blum, and told him tales of the building industry. He had once worked on a building site in the summer holidays, and it still came in useful. At Aschaffenburg the TV quiz man rose, took his large tome and said goodbye.

"I'm going to have a bit of a lie-down before we reach Wiesbaden. Watch the show on April the fifth! No, no, don't get up – and thanks a lot!"

Blum asked for his bill. He felt a pressing need to shut himself in the toilet or pull the emergency brake, but he stayed where he was, drank another coffee, and watched as the train rolled on into the chemicals-producing area, where the sky was green as grass.

14

No one met Blum, no one had laid on a stormy reception for him, no one took any interest in him at all except for a foreign gentleman in a turban and a voluminous white robe who held a city street map under his nose, and was greatly disappointed when Blum told him, "I'm a stranger here myself." And Frankfurt was indeed strange to him, although he had once known the city very well. At eye level there were still places he remembered, but everything over ten feet high seemed to be new. Banks, boutiques, brothels, and two pharmacies on every corner – anyone who didn't make money here, thought Blum, didn't need it.

He left his sample case and travelling bag in a left-luggage locker on level B under the central police station. It was now five-thirty. He didn't look for a hotel – if all went smoothly he might be able to spend the night at the airport and catch the first flight to Miami in the morning. Or to Maracaibo. Or Macao. He went to the toilet and hid the key to the left-luggage locker in his left boot (luckily he usually bought his footwear half a size too large), and then he called the dealer. It took him some time to find a working phone, and the fuggy atmosphere was beginning to get to him by the time he finally reached the man on the other end of the line. He sounded nervous and suspicious, and wouldn't let Blum say anything.

"Know your way around Frankfurt?"

"Of course."

"Then we'll meet at the Iron Bridge in half an hour."

The gulls were screaming above the river Main. Pleasure boats bobbed up and down by the bank. The river was high, and oily water slapped against the planks of their hulls. Old women stood in the public gardens and on the bridge feeding pigeons and gulls, and Turkish children were playing counting-out games or Ayatollah. Blum admired the skyline. Say what you like, they knew what they were doing in Frankfurt, and even if the scene in general made you want to puke, at least they showed you how to puke profitably here.

At 18.06 hours precisely Blum heard someone cough behind him: the man who was big in the trade was a tall, thin youth of twenty-two at the most, who obviously shaved only twice a week. He had carefully styled fairish hair and an arrogant set to his mouth. His eyes were constantly moving, and he took his hands out of the pockets of his white raincoat only if he absolutely had to. He wore an unobtrusively expensive cashmere scarf around his neck. He examined Blum for a moment, then nodded gloomily and jerked his head in the direction of the bridge.

"We can talk better up there."

Up on the bridge an unpleasantly cold wind was blowing through the rust-corroded iron arches. The dealer kept his hands in his raincoat pockets, and watched Blum freezing in his silk shirt and blazer with the elegant cravat.

"I know it's cold," he said, "but we won't be overheard up here. How much high C do you have?"

Good Lord, thought Blum, you're pretty advanced for your age.

"Five pounds," he said. "Five pounds of Peruvian flake, 96 per cent, straight from the producer. So strong it'd eat your nose away. But the brunette will have told you that."

The tall man smiled down at Blum. It was a rather frosty smile.

"Quite right, no names. And how much do you want for it?"

"A hundred and fifty grand, in cash."

By now they had walked over the bridge once. Layabouts were lounging around at the far end, passing a bottle from hand to hand. They turned. The dealer stopped now and then and acted as if he were pointing out the city landmarks to Blum.

"That's crazy," he said. "And over there you see the cathedral. I can get five kilos for 150 grand. If you want to make that kind of money you'll have to sell it on the street. The East Harbour is over there."

"I could make half a million on the street," said Blum, trying to light a cigarette. "A hundred and fifty grand is a realistic price. Once you've cut it you'll make twice that out of my stuff, and hey presto, there's your five kilos. I told you, Peruvian flake. The best."

"I really prefer Bolivian," said the tall man. "It's got more subtlety."

"I thought you were going to flog it."

"All gone," an old woman called to the gulls that had been snapping her breadcrusts out of the air. "All gone! Nothing left!" She stuffed the empty plastic bag in her shopping carrier. Blum had finally lit his HB and responded to her mad grin as best he could.

"They've all got cancer," said the dealer. "And the latest skyscraper – yes, look over there – that's the Deutsche Bank." Then, lowering his voice: "We might start talking at 80,000."

They had reached the end of the bridge again, and turned.

"Who's got cancer? The old women or the seagulls?"

"The women, the gulls, all of them. Don't you have cancer too?"

"No," said Blum.

"You just don't know it yet."

"Do you?"

"Well, no, but I've already had four stomach ulcers."

"Is dealing so stressful?"

"My work is stressful. I deal in coke on the side just to make up for it." He looked gloomily at Blum. "I expect you thought I was around twenty. As a matter of fact I'm twenty-six. Been in advertising for seven years."

"Amazing," said Blum, "but all the same I want 150."

It had grown too cold for the layabouts, and they had moved on to Sachsenhausen. The dealer turned again. Blum was beginning to puff and pant. He wasn't used to this kind of fitness training.

"If your C is really that good – and I'm always sceptical about Peruvian – we might be able to agree on ninety. I'll have to try it first, of course."

Blum threw his cigarette away. A gull snapped it up.

"Then let's go. I have some with me."

The tall man looked at him distrustfully. "You mean now? Why are you in such a hurry?"

"What do you mean, a hurry? I need the money."

"I believe you. But a deal over five pounds of snow isn't done that quickly. I'd have to see it all first and choose what I test for myself. You might give me your Peruvian flake now, and then the rest turns out to be washing powder. Nothing doing."

I ought to push you into the Main, thought Blum, that's where you belong, down in its murky waters. He stopped. The other man held on to his hairstyle.

"No wonder you have stomach ulcers. You're over-suspicious, that's what it is."

"Anyone can see you're new to the trade. I don't really do business with novices, but if your stuff is really so great . . . I tell you what: where can I reach you?"

They were back on the Frankfurt side of the river again, and the tall man was getting restless.

"Nowhere," said Blum. "I'll ring you."

That seemed to make sense to this character. "Give me the sample, then. But not so's the whole of Frankfurt can see you."

Once again, Blum had no choice – holding his breath, he gave the man the little bag he had prepared.

"Call me tomorrow morning and we'll see what we can do."

"Not likely," said Blum, quite loud. "You'll have a nice evening with my stuff and I'll be left high and dry. Do your test now, and I'll call you at eight and we'll get everything in the clear."

"Can't be done," said the tall man, straightening his cashmere scarf. "I have a meeting at eight. Try around midnight, but I can't promise anything."

A white Mercedes drew up by the kerb, with a red-haired woman at the wheel. The dealer drove off in the car. A Turkish boy pointed a broomstick at Blum, crooking his little finger. "You dead!" he said, and laughed. When he saw Blum's face he ran away.

15

Blum was sitting in a café, seeing ghosts. Hadn't Rossi pressed close to him as he walked along a dark side street on his way to the central police station? There was a car parked outside the café with a woman and two men in it – Renée, her husband and his gay friend? And now he came to think of it, he'd known several of the people in the café ever since Tangiers, where he once dealt briefly in stolen passports. Wherever he went they were sitting there already, staring at him through their dark glasses, and he stared back at them through his own dark glasses, but there were always more of them and they could stare for longer. Oh, hell, said Blum to himself, ordering another cognac, you just don't have any luck. You've finally dumped yourself right in it with that five pounds of charlie. Keeping your nose clean for forty years – that business with the European Community butter was perfectly legal, and after all, he'd never actually claimed that the Titian was genuine – and any high-class supermarket sells porn magazines these days – and now he had go and get mixed up with the drugs trade. Ten years behind bars was the best he could expect. And that would mean the end of his life as such. He remembered the horror of it back in Istanbul, and he'd been entirely innocent. But if he hadn't happened to have a few banknotes of large denominations he'd still be in that dump today. He shuddered, and with trembling hands reached for the glass the waitress put down in front of him. To her, thought Blum, I'm still just your average type with cirrhosis of the liver, or Blum of the textiles industry who went bust yesterday and is going to shoot himself after the next cognac.

And now another flesh-and-blood ghost came through the door, making itself out to be a Pakistani by the name of Hassan Abdul Haq. In fact four versions of the ghost came in at once; three of them looked rather like Mr Haq, and one of them was exactly like him, down to every greasy strand of hair and every fibre in his green artificial silk suit. The ghost saw Blum, came over to him, smiling, and showed him Mr Haq's two gold teeth.

"Mr Blum! What a surprise!"

It was indeed Mr Haq. He whispered to his countrymen, directed them to an empty table, and came back to Blum.

"May I sit down here a moment?"

"By all means, Mr Haq. I must say it's a surprise for me to see you here too."

"Ah, but I told you I had to visit Germany because of Jeddah, remember?"

"You didn't mention Frankfurt."

"But Frankfurt is in Germany, right, Mr Blum? Surely one could say it was in Germany!"

"All the same, I didn't expect to see you here. Anyone else, but not you. Can I order you something?"

It proved unnecessary. Mr Haq seemed to be known in this café – the waitress was already bringing him a pot of tea. Curiously enough, here in Frankfurt a determination that Blum had not noticed in Malta emanated from the little Pakistani. This time he was wearing a narrow black tie with the white shirt that Blum had seen on a hanger in Valletta. How familiar someone seemed when you'd seen his shirt on a hanger, and the remains of shampoo in his wash-basin with the hairs still in them. Blum ordered a double mocha.

"Won't you invite your fellow countrymen over to our table, Mr Haq?"

"My fellow countrymen can stay put. They don't speak our language, if you see what I mean."

Blum piled sugar into his coffee.

"You shouldn't take so much sugar, Mr Blum," said the Pakistani. "Sugar is very bad for you."

"An unusual opinion for an Oriental, Mr Haq, if I may say so."

"If we ate less sugar we might have solved our problems as well as you have. That, of course, was a joke, Mr Blum."

"Of course."

"But there's a grain of truth in every joke, don't you think?"

"Mm. But since you mentioned speaking the same language, Mr Haq, do you remember the evening you came to my hotel?"

"Yes, of course. It was only three days ago."

"Really? How time flies . . ."

Blum described the robbery in Republic Street. Mr Haq looked shocked.

"You surely don't think that I —?"

"No, I don't. I admit I suspected you briefly, but the magazines weren't realistic enough for you."

"Are you getting hold of new magazines now?"

"No. I have something else on the go." Blum stubbed out his cigarette and looked the Pakistani in the eye. "Remember you said you could use a man like me?"

"Why, yes, Mr Blum. In Jeddah."

"Well, Mr Haq, this evening I'm saying it's possible *I* could use someone like *you*."

Mr Haq cautiously sipped his tea and gave Blum a look that was older than Pakistan, as old as any deal done between human beings.

"I'm honoured, of course, Mr Blum," he said. "But what exactly could I do for you?"

Blum looked round for anyone observing him. The whole café was full of observers. Even Mr Haq's countrymen were staring openly at them.

"Let's go somewhere else, Mr Haq. I'm inviting you to dinner. Somewhere we won't be disturbed."

Mr Haq looked concerned, and glanced at his watch, which gleamed gold.

"I'm afraid that won't be possible, Mr Blum. As you can see, my countrymen . . . well, we have something to discuss this evening. And unfortunately it's already late! But why not come to my hotel tomorrow, and then we can talk at leisure."

Blum noted down the address on a paper napkin.

"Of course I can't be sure you'll find me there, Mr Blum, I have so much to do at the moment . . . but do try, say around mid-day, perhaps for lunch? Good evening, Mr Blum, it's been such a pleasure to see you again!"

Then they disappeared into the night, Mr Haq and his three companions, and Blum left too. The car with the woman and two men in it had gone. He called the dealer from a telephone kiosk. The answering machine replied. "There is no one available to take your call at the moment," said a sexless voice. "Please leave a message and we will call you back."

"A hundred and twenty grand," said Blum, hanging up. He retrieved his travelling bag from the left-luggage locker and found a hotel on the outskirts of the station district. He ate a shashlik with potato salad in the snack bar opposite, and then lay down with a small bottle of Cutty Sark and his Bahamas handbook on the bed in the narrow room, with its wallpaper the colour of pea soup, its dripping tap, its blue bedside lamp, its yellow coconut-fibre carpet, the Merian engraving above the desk, and the groaning and squealing of the bedstead next door. He took a bath and got out of the tub feeling exhausted. He rang again. The dealer wasn't there. He left the number of the hotel. Then he stuck the locker key under the wardrobe with sticky tape. He poured himself another whisky, using the tooth-glass. Everything smelled of Odol. Sirens were howling. He switched the radio on. It was playing Bert Kaempfert, "Spanish Eyes".

16

Blum waited all Tuesday for the dealer to call back. No call came. In the afternoon he bought several paperbacks and a large bottle of Cutty Sark. After dinner he tried to read in his room, but after a while he fell asleep over his book. Later, a collision down in the street at the junction woke him: two cars, a hollow crashing sound, metal, glass, police cars, the ambulance was sent off, onlookers soon dispersed. He drank a whisky. No call. Without a return phone call it would be no use for him to visit Mr Haq either. He wanted a woman, and found himself counting his money. Could he afford the 100 marks for a tart? He had just under DM 1,700. And of course his sample case in the locker. It would have to stay there another night. Was the locker secure enough? He went over to the central police station. A few uniformed officers were around, but they were taking no notice of anyone but the shady characters being brought in. He fed more money into the slot of the locker. Blum no longer felt fear, only a sense of paralysis that made every movement difficult, as if he were suffering from consumption.

He went back to the hotel, stuck the locker key to the inside of the lavatory cistern, stared at his money. He was going to be forty next week, and here he was in this room in a run-down hotel, unable to turn five pounds of cocaine into ready cash. And if he did, then what? He saw himself at forty-three, at forty-seven, at fifty-two, in other rooms, but all of them alike, with a shirt drying on a hanger, a fly buzzing against the lamp, a radio playing "Spanish Eyes", sirens howling, the level of whisky in the bottle going down, his heart-beats coming faster, and a telephone that didn't ring. He went downstairs again and crossed the street for a shashlik and a beer. A drunk had laid his head on the bar and was sobbing. Two elderly tarts with fat legs under their gaudy miniskirts were dancing together. An American was feeding the fruit machine, and when he won he bought an Underberg and put it in front of the drunk, who raised his head and assured everyone, in tears, that he hadn't done his old lady in but he'd ruined his stomach with Underberg. Then he drank the Underberg and put his head down on the bar again. The tarts stationed themselves in front of Blum, wiggling their hips, and he bought them a couple of vodkas, went to the all-night pharmacy, purchased a number of bromine tablets and went back to the hotel to sleep.

The phone call came next morning when Blum was sitting in the breakfast room with a throbbing head, drinking the weak coffee and reading a newspaper report about asylum seekers getting their teeth fixed at the taxpayers' expense.

"Sorry, I had to go to Milan yesterday, didn't get back until one in the morning. I suggest we have lunch."

They met at a clip-joint near the hotel. The dealer lunched on four Alka Seltzers, a sesame seed roll with steak tartare, and a Bloody Mary, extra strong. Blum had the full menu at DM 29.90. The leg of veal was just enough for three forkfuls. The dealer was wearing a yellow linen double-breasted suit, a pink tie and white shoes with black toecaps. He seemed to have done a lot of shopping in Milan.

"Mightn't we be overheard in here?" asked Blum, sipping his Budweiser.

The dealer stroked back his hair and looked at Blum with amusement. He seemed to be in a good mood.

"This place belongs to us," he said.

"Us?"

"A couple of friends and me."

"Ah, then you won't have any trouble with our little transaction."

"That depends entirely on you. Your high C is good stuff all right – always supposing the whole five pounds are like what I tested – but even 120 grand isn't a realistic basis for negotiation. You surely must see that."

"I think it is," said Blum, spreading butter on a slice of rye bread. The butter, of course, was chilled hard, and the bread crumbled.

"You're not seeing this the right way, I'm afraid," said the dealer, looking with distaste at the wrecked slice of bread. "There's a glut here right now, and the market isn't big enough yet to absorb everything."

"First, I don't believe it, and second, I'm not interested. My price is 120 grand, and I'm not going below that."

The dealer ordered another Bloody Mary. Blum pushed his plate aside, looked round in vain for a toothpick, and finally used a match. The dealer stared at him for a while and then lit a cigarillo. The conversation had reached deadlock. The dealer would go no higher than 85,000, otherwise, he said, he saw no profit worth mentioning. Blum was not giving way. He felt that he mustn't. When you've been thinking in terms of 480 grand you can't go below 100. After all, you had your reputation to think of, and even if you didn't have much of a reputation you still had your self-respect.

"Well now, Herr Blum . . ."

"How come you suddenly know my name?"

"The name Blum is quite well known in Munich. But you're right, let's leave names out of this. If you'd rather risk selling it on the street . . . well, I suggest you open a little stall. You'll see how long you live that way."

Blum didn't like it, but there was no point in stonewalling any longer. The tall man was his only contact. It was time to close the deal.

"All right, I'll go halfway to meet you. Let's agree on a round figure. A hundred thousand marks."

"Done," said the dealer. "We'll meet here tomorrow evening at six-thirty and drive over to Oberrad. I have an apartment there. It'll be safe."

Oh yes, so you'll be taking me for a ride, thought Blum. You think it won't be difficult. While the tall man was paying the bill he went out. The weather had changed; there was a cold wind with showers of rain.

"I'm not too keen on that idea," said Blum, when the other man joined him in the street. "I've been thinking. I'd be on your home ground. That's not secure enough for me."

The tall man frowned. It made him look twenty-three.

"A little trust is part of the deal."

"Yes, but not on my side."

"Listen, after all I have a business to run . . ."

"That never stopped anyone cutting a few corners too."

"You're an odd fish, I must say. Right, then, think up something else. But we meet here at six-thirty. Do you have a car?"

"I'll get hold of one." Blum had one more question. "Tell me, why do you do this? I mean, with your advertising agency, your restaurant – why risk so long in jail for your high C? Are you so fond of money?"

The tall man climbed into his Mercedes, and then looked at Blum once more. He was smiling. Now he looked only seventeen. "It's fun," he said, and closed the car door.

17

"A nice room, Mr Blum – by comparison with Valletta."

The Pakistani pushed the chair with its worn upholstery over to Blum, and sat on the bed himself.

"Very nice, Mr Haq. May I ask what you're paying for this delightful spot?"

The delightful spot was a dark room on the fourth floor of a mid-nineteenth-century building with a view of a large filling station. The ground, third and fourth floors belonged to the Pension Waldfrieden – the Woodland Peace Boarding House, although there was no sign of any woodland. The name probably dated as far back as the furniture. Mr Haq at least seemed to feel at ease with the German oak cabinet and wardrobe and the wash-stand with its flowered enamel bowl. The one modern piece was an electric hotplate, on which Mr Haq was cooking a meal.

"You were invited yesterday, Mr Blum, but of course you're very welcome today too. I hope you like curry. I'm afraid I can't offer you any of the iced drinks you're used to, but perhaps they'll have cooled off in the fresh air."

He went to the window, opened it, and brought in a bottle of beer and an open bottle of Coca-Cola.

"There, you see – the cold weather has its uses. I'm not paying much more here than in the Cumberland, *and* I have a bathroom. Beer or cola, Mr Blum?"

"If you had a tea . . ."

"Oh, you'd like tea? I always have tea around, Mr Blum."

He poured Blum a glass of tea. It was even hot.

"Thank you, Mr Haq. Didn't you have a bathroom at the Cumberland, then?"

"In theory, Mr Blum, purely in theory. The bathroom was being renovated."

"I see."

"Do you like your curry medium or hot, Mr Blum?"

"I've already eaten, thank you."

"Hot, then."

The Pakistani added more ingredients to the pan. The aroma was like that of the Pegasus Bar on Thursdays, only considerably stronger. Mr Haq had his suit on again, but with a sports shirt under it and slippers on his feet. He had made himself comfortable.

"It won't taste as good as my wife's, Mr Blum, but I hope it will be edible."

"You're married?"

"I'm not a young man any more, Mr Blum." He discreetly spared Blum the same question. "You really must visit me in Lahore some time. Lahore, as of course you know, is the most important city in Central Asia. You can eat at my home and get your drinks in the Punjab Club. It's the most fashionable club in all Pakistan, they say. Do you play billiards? Yes, of course you do. The best billiards of all are played in the Punjab Club."

The easterner had an inexhaustible talent for elaborate conversation. It was some time before he allowed Blum to come to the point. Blum kept it short, and confined himself to hints.

"But what could I do for you in this matter, Mr Blum? As I told you in the café, my opportunities here are very limited."

Blum reminded him of the loss of his porn magazines. "You'll understand that I've been rather nervous since then . . ."

The Pakistani forced a polite smile.

"And you think my humble self could keep a robber at bay?"

"No, this is something quite different, Mr Haq. We're dealing with absolutely straight people. But it would just be better if I turned up with company to complete this transaction."

"I see. There must be a considerable sum involved?"

"The amount isn't so important. It's more a matter of – of honour."

"Ah. A contingency not unknown to me. But tell me one thing, Mr Blum – don't you have friends in this city?"

"It's not my home town."

"Remarkable. I'd have thought a man like you had friends everywhere. I mean, this is your own country."

"You're forgetting how long I've been away."

"Only a year, Mr Blum. A year – and you have no friends left! No family either? Everyone has family . . ."

Blum felt the conversation slipping out of his grasp.

"Of course I'd reimburse you for your trouble."

"Oh, please, Mr Blum! We're friends in a way, we speak the same language. Now let's eat."

He fetched plates from the wall cupboard. They were heavy stoneware, chipped all round the edges. Mr Haq served the curry.

"Say if it's too hot for you."

"It's excellent. My compliments."

"Oh, that's nothing, Mr Blum. Of course I could have taken you to a restaurant, but I'm afraid we wouldn't have got a really good curry. Now in Lahore . . ."

After they had eaten, Mr Haq returned to the subject.

"You see, I'd like to oblige you, Mr Blum, particularly in an affair of honour, but on the other hand I wouldn't like to break the laws of the country where I am a guest . . ."

"Mr Haq, if you're at all afraid of breaking laws . . . you'd be risking far less than in your beloved Saudi Arabia."

Saudi Arabia was the cue Mr Haq had been waiting for. Once again Blum had to listen to him describing the ease of making money there. Money practically grew on the trees, he said, or rather, as no trees grew there it spurted up from the sand . . .

"I thought," said Blum, "you had a nice little earner of some kind over here."

"Oh, that's only peanuts, as the Americans say, Mr Blum. One is glad to help if one can. 'What you give is given for the sake of your souls,' says the Prophet. But how can one give if one doesn't have enough oneself? No, my countrymen must change their way of thinking. They must realize that they'll be better off in Saudi Arabia than here. Because, Mr Blum, the competition is just too great in this country of yours. Don't you agree?"

"Possibly," said Blum. Finally they got around to discussing the fee. For DM 2,000 Mr Haq was prepared to break a few harmless laws of the country in which he was at present residing in order to help his friend Blum, for the sake of appearances, in a transaction which principally if not entirely concerned a point of honour. Blum would pay an advance of DM 500. Mr Haq was not to be moved on that point.

On the stairs Blum encountered a whole troop of Orientals. Many of them wore turbans, and they all greeted him with deference. So this was the important business friend of the eminent Mr Hassan Abdul

Haq of Lahore! A great dealer in Western artworks. I must be out of my mind, thought Blum. I should have gone to Hackensack. Crazy, these easterners. But was Hackensack a practicable alternative? Chemicals and information, Mr Blum. Oh, sure, Mr Hackensack. The curry had been good.

18

Time seemed to have stood still in the jazz cellar. Blum had last been there twelve years ago, but except for the seating and the prices nothing had changed. The same faces, the same conversations, the same music. The trombonist had become world-famous, but he was still a middle-aged man making music for other middle-aged men, melancholy and fed up.

These people seemed to have everything they needed, and if not, then they didn't let it show. At least, Charlie Parker had died far away from here. Jazz and coke, they were still around, but not for these people. They'd papered over the cracks with mortgage contracts, electoral action groups, grants and wedding rings – the cracks through which, perhaps, they had once seen what was really out there. Well, what was that to him? He'd be away from here tomorrow evening, he just had to get through tonight and tomorrow, and then he might be thinking about a mortgage in Bombay himself, or playing a game of billiards in the Punjab Club. Mr Haq had mentioned a daughter. Or was it two daughters?

He watched a blonde making her way from table to table, apparently in search of someone. Or no, perhaps she was after something else. People reacted with annoyance. Didn't want their subdued drone of conversation to be disturbed. Good figure, thought Blum, almost voluptuous, and a mouth reminiscent of Bardot, but a Bardot gone to seed. She wore a fake fur coat open in front, and under it a black overshirt, old jeans, boots with silver lacquer flaking off them, and a shoulder-bag. At one point she looked in his direction. He sketched a smile. She turned away and talked to a man at the bar. Then she disappeared. Fair enough. He ordered another vodka and tonic. Once he'd flogged the coke he could afford something rather more chic. Gradually the customers dispersed, and the blonde suddenly reappeared. She clearly hadn't found whatever she was looking for. When she glanced at him this time, those full lips formed into a smile which he returned. The hair too, he thought, that's almost like BB. She actually came over to him. My God, this is ridiculous, a youthful dream.

"Can I sit here for a moment? I wanted to ask you something."

Blum pulled out the chair for her. At close quarters the fake fur seemed a little moth-eaten, and she didn't look quite so good herself, but what you could see of her, and perhaps even more what you couldn't, suggested a heated, lively temperament. Blum cleared his throat, but she was already going on.

"May I have one of your cigarettes? HB, oh well, better than nothing." She spoke a neutral big-city German with a trace of south German accent. Her voice sounded slightly husky, as if she hadn't quite recovered from a cough. "I was going to ask if I can sleep with you?"

"Sleep with me?"

"Well, spend the night at your place, know what I mean? I can give you some shit if you want. You must have an apartment somewhere, and they chucked me out of my room in the place where I was sharing three days ago because I was going to leave anyway, so I didn't see why I should pay the full rent. Anyway they're so stupid there, understand?"

"You want to spend the night with me?"

Blum stared at her. Was she a decoy? But the CID wouldn't go to those lengths, and the cartels could afford something smarter. He smiled again.

"What's your name?"

"Cora. What's yours?"

"Blum. Like a flower in bloom. Well, look, Cora, I'm no Jack the Ripper, and I don't have a wife to make objections, but I'm afraid I don't have an apartment either, only a hotel room. I'm just passing through."

She pushed a strand of hair back from her brow. Strictly speaking it was ash-blonde hair, but ash blonde is still blonde.

"Passing through, I see. Typical, just my luck. But maybe your hotel room is big enough. I mean, I don't have much baggage. Where is it, then – the Intercontinental?"

"Not exactly. What'll you have to drink?"

"I'd rather have something to eat, if you don't mind. I've only had a few chips all day."

"Broke?"

She nodded and looked piercingly at him. Her eyes were rather large: cool and grey.

"Then let's go and get something proper to eat."

"I still have to find a place to sleep, though . . ."

"That'll be okay."

"You think so?"

She stood up, and those breasts curved out right before his eyes. She really did look a little like the early BB, and somehow more voluptuous.

The only place to eat that was still open was an Onkel Max. They sat among the drunks and ate Wiener schnitzel, or rather Cora ate Wiener schnitzel while Blum slowly drank a beer and watched her. He liked a girl with a good appetite. "How old are you, Cora?"

"Do you have to know? Not quite thirty yet. Are you sure you don't have a first name?"

"Blum sounds better."

"Come on, tell me."

"Listen, my name's Blum."

"Okay, just as you like. And how old are you?"

"Not quite forty yet."

"Then we go well together."

"How do you mean?"

She had finished eating and lit a cigarette. He had given her three marks for Roth-Händle. She smoked as hard as she ate.

"For the night," she said. "You have to go well together even for one night. Oh, do take those sunglasses off, they look silly, you're not in the Mafia. Your eyes are okay. Almost green. Eyes are so important, nice eyes. Mine are a bit too big, don't you think? What are you looking at? *Are* you in the Mafia?"

He put the glasses back on. There was no point. He couldn't drag this girl into it. Perhaps the guys the coke belonged to would strike tonight, or perhaps the cops were on his track and already waiting for him back at the hotel.

"Listen, Cora, I'll give you fifty marks and you can get yourself a hotel room . . ."

"Why? I thought I could sleep with you . . ."

"I didn't say so."

"Oh, I thought you did. Well, never mind. But I'm not taking money from you, I mean, that's crazy. I'll find something else. Or I can just sleep in the park."

"Do sit down, Cora."

"I'll go when it suits me."

But she sat down again, inhaled on her cigarette and puffed out a thick cloud of smoke. It's all one to her, thought Blum. No room, no money, wandering around

101

the streets, talking to men, and she probably has enough stuff in her bag to land her in the loony bin. She's not afraid of the Rossis and Renées of this world either. True enough, there was something that bothered him about this picture; perhaps the colours were laid on a bit too thick here and there. But another night alone in that bleak room . . .

"The fact is," he said cautiously, "things could get rather lively in my room tonight."

She grinned meaningfully.

"Not the way you think," he said. "Something like superior forces at work."

"We're helpless against superior forces, isn't that right, Blum?"

"The bill, please, waiter."

They took a taxi. Blum had the impression that they were being followed, but there was nothing to be done about it. Anyone who wanted to find him could find him. Where could he hide? You can't hide with five pounds of coke, not if you want to make money out of it. And now he'd landed himself with a blonde too, a tarty blonde pot-head, probably with the police after her, but she was what he wanted. At twenty he'd dreamed of such blondes and jerked himself off. Now at forty he finally had one, even if she was shop-soiled and run-down. But it was never too late for blondes.

19

"Hey, this is really stylish," said Cora, when they were in his hotel room. Blum had give the night porter a twenty.

"What's so stylish about it?"

"Well, I mean, even a bathroom. Almost like in the Intercontinental. Do you think I could have a bath now?"

Before he could reply she kissed him fleetingly on the mouth and then disappeared into the bathroom with her bag. He heard the water running. The bed next door squealed again, and there was a noise in the room above as if someone were pushing the wardrobe back and forth. Blum poured himself a small Cutty Sark, sat by the window and stared out into the street. Two drunks, a police car, showers of rain. The light of the street lamps was reflected back from the bank façades. Why shouldn't he strike lucky for once? Another sixteen hours. He switched the radio on. A smoky alto voice sang:

> "When the day has turned
> to evenin' . . . baby
> and the stars are out
> to show their magic
> that's the time you feel
> so lonesome
> it's so strange and blue
> 'round midnight . . ."

When Cora came out of the bathroom she was wearing nothing but her overshirt and lilac panties. Her wet hair fell to her shoulders, and Blum saw that she had made up her eyes. She had a smoking joint in her hand.

"Want a drag?"

Blum shook his head. She hadn't dried herself. Water was running down her legs and trickling into the coconut-fibre carpet, which turned dark. She had strong, shapely legs. She was strong and shapely in general. In five years' time she'd have weight problems, but at the moment everything was just the way Blum liked it. She sat down on the bed.

"Anyone would think you wanted to seduce me," said Blum. "A bath, a joint, bare legs . . ."

"There's only one bed here, after all," she said. "It'll be better if we fancy each other."

"Do you fancy me?"

She blew a cloud of hashish in his direction and narrowed her eyes.

"Can't see much of you right now. But I guess I might if you were a bit more forthcoming. Sure you don't want a drag?"

Blum's expression was gloomy. He did not particularly like hash, and anyway it was about time to find out why this woman was sitting on his bed.

"Who set you on to me, baby?"

She placed the remnants of the joint in the ashtray and stared at him. Her face coarsened, and she looked like a country slut come to town for the dancing but ready to slap down anyone who takes liberties.

"I don't understand, Blum," she said hoarsely.

"You understand perfectly well. Who was it? Rossi? The syndicate? Hermes? Renée? That shady adman here in Frankfurt? Come on, tell me. You're from Munich, aren't you? I can tell from your voice."

104

He had jumped up and gone to the bathroom before she could answer. The key was still inside the cistern. Her things were lying around, her bag, one of those Moroccan leather jobs, was under the wash-basin on which she had laid out her makeup. He picked up the bag and looked inside it.

"What do you expect to find in there?" She was standing in the doorway, smoking again, Roth-Händle this time. "A pistol? A kilo of heroin? You've been watching too many gangster films, if you ask me. Or are you really in the underworld? Did you nick stuff from them and now they're after you?"

He dropped the bag. She reached for him, pulled him towards her and looked into his face at close quarters. Seeming to see the fear there, she dropped her cigarette and embraced him, pressed him to her with her damp hair on his shirt, her damp mouth on his face. After a while he pushed her gently away.

"Pick that cigarette end up, Cora. Hotel fires can be pretty unpleasant."

She smiled and picked up the smouldering cigarette end. The curves of her lilac-clad buttocks swelled. He went into the bedroom, sat down by the window again and drank his whisky. She lay on the bed and listened as he told her the broad outlines of the story.

"So you think one of them planted me on you?"

"Could be. I mean, it's an elegant solution – we screw, you pretend to be asleep, and when I wake up, assuming I ever wake up at all, you're off and away with the snow. To whoever sent you."

"If you go on like that you'll have me scared too."

"Why did you approach me in the jazz cellar?"

"I thought I told you."

"Tell me your story."

"I don't have one."

"Oh, come on, everyone has a story: let's hear all about your childhood in the orphanage, your marriage, your suicide attempts . . ."

"I don't like that kind of story. You don't need to know anything about me. I didn't want to know anything about you either until you started acting so crazy."

"Have you been in jail? The nuthouse? You must come from somewhere. You must have done something."

"I've lived, same as you. You think only men can live as they like?"

"Oh, very well, I'll find out some time. And what do you want to do now?"

"Before you flipped —"

"Me, flipped?"

"— I was going to sleep. Maybe even with you." She looked at him, and then past him. "Got any of that snow with you? The night will soon be over."

So she was a coke-head after all. He hesitated. He liked her. She had some style, and she was right, the night would soon be over. After all, he must try the stuff himself some time, and who with if not her? And when if not now? He removed his ankleboots and took the bag out of his pocket. She gave him her make-up mirror, and he tipped a pinch of powder on the glass. Cora knelt beside him, her arms wrapped round her legs. Her face was gleaming.

"Hey, that looks good, Blum."

"Peruvian flake, top quality. Have you often snorted?"

"Can't often afford to. But I know people who deal in it. If you're looking for buyers, I guess they'd be interested."

"I have a buyer," he said. They hadn't yet discussed that point. He carefully cleaned his nose.

"Go on."

"Looks like you can't wait, right? Are you an addict?"

"You don't get addicted to cocaine, Blum. Cocaine means other kinds of problems. You ought to know that."

She watched him snort two lines. He waited until he felt the tingling in his head as the flakes reached his body, then lit a cigarette. Cora put the mirror on her knee and snorted the other two lines. Then she closed her eyes and put her head down between her legs, hands on her ankles. Blum looked down on her breasts as they rose and fell. There was rather a lot of them. She took his hand with the cigarette, kissed the palm, took a deep pull and slowly blew the smoke over his fingers. Then she took his socks off and massaged his feet. Her fingers were cool. His member swelled and pressed against the nape of her neck. He began stroking her shoulders with his left hand, and had reached her breasts when she closed her eyes, put her head right back on his swollen, throbbing penis and said, "Come on, let's snort a little more."

They snorted a little more. This time Blum couldn't sit still. He rose, walked up and down the room, alternately drank a sip of water and some whisky, lit two cigarettes at once, made his way into the bathroom, examined himself intently in the mirror, put his tongue out – everything fine, nice and pink, not coated. Then he stared out of the window again. Outside, there were faint grey edges to the darkness. The first tram rattled around the corner. Cora was lying in the armchair all this time, one bare leg over its arm, hands behind her head, eyes sometimes closed, sometimes looking at Blum, who took off his shirt and lit his tenth cigarette.

"How are you doing, Blum?"

"Fine," he grunted.

"It always makes me feel so peaceful. I like it that you don't keep talking. Other people rabbit on for hours."

"Not me," said Blum, who would have liked nothing better.

"You don't look peaceful, though."

"That's just appearances. I can see it all clear as day – the whole thing. The connections, understand?"

"What connections?"

"Oh God, it all hangs together. Everything."

"You and me too?"

"Sure, you and me too. The way it all worked out – when I think of Malta—"

She stretched her arms out to him.

"Come on, show me the connection."

From the chair, the coconut-fibre carpet and the bedside rug they moved to the bed, clinging together, drenched in sweat, Cora with her pubic hair damp, her eyelids smeared green, Blum gasping, *in extremis*.

"Now, now, now," cried Cora, but he couldn't come. She kissed his penis, which was standing out from his body, hard and quivering, she stroked his thighs.

"I can't come," he murmured.

"Yes, you can. You can."

Overhead a radio was switched on, full volume, music for morning exercises. A woman's voice said: "And now we crouch down, we loosen up our hips, with a left two three, and a right two three." Then someone hammered on the wall and the radio was turned down. Blum laughed. His throat was burning. He switched off the light and they lay side by side, sweating into the bedclothes.

"Do you think it's possible, Blum?"

"Of course. Sure. Everything's possible. I don't know. Why not?"

"I mean are *we* possible?"

He said nothing. What did she mean? He heard sea-gulls screaming. Gulls were possible. You lay on the beach exhausted, among the empty cans and crusts of bread, and suddenly they were over you. That was possible.

Cora sighed, rubbed his penis over her breasts, pressed one nipple to the slit, wound strands of her hair around the glans, licked them off, laughed, reached for the cocaine, tipped a trail of bluish snow on his penis and slid it into her. Something exploded in his head, the sky was rent apart, the gulls dived into the sea, Cora screamed, screamed, screamed, and Blum came.

20

When Blum woke up a few hours later Cora was still lying at the other end of the bed. She had a sketchpad on her knees and was chewing a pencil.

"Slept well, Blum?"

"Not too bad," he said. "How about you? Haven't you had any sleep?"

She looked tired. The cold sunlight coming in through the window put ten years on her age.

"I had a dream, and it woke me up, and then I did some drawing. I like to draw, you see. To me it's like meditating or yoga. Or praying."

"What did you dream?"

"I never remember my dreams."

"I don't believe you. That's not the way you look."

"How do I look, then?"

"Well, good."

It sounded feeble. He felt feeble too. He patted her leg and crawled out of bed. The room looked wrecked, and the Roth-Händle smoke clung to the ceiling like smog. He glanced at the time. Ten-thirty. Time to visit Mr Haq. He made his way into the bathroom, drank a pint of tap-water and showered. After shaving he felt almost like a man of thirty-nine again. He got dressed.

"I have something to do, Cora. Will you stay here till I come back?"

She seemed to be entirely absorbed in her sketching, and it was only after a while that she said, without raising her head, "How much are you asking for the stuff?"

He was just buttoning up his navy-blue shirt. He hesitated for a moment, and then said, "I'll get 100,000 marks for it." There was no reason not to tell her. Maybe he'd even take her away with him – for a while.

At that she raised her head and smiled incredulously. Or rather, she just thrust her lips out.

"For five pounds of this stuff?"

"Yes, not bad. A hundred thousand smackers." It sounded good in the circumstances, in this bleak room. "In cash, too."

"That's nothing like enough, Blum. You can make far more out of this stuff."

"Yes, sure. I thought so too. But don't forget I'm in a hurry. I want to get away from here. I'm not keen to spend weeks on end trudging around Frankfurt with my sample case, selling the stuff off in little bags. I want to get out as fast as I can, and I'll be happy if I get 100 grand this evening. The day after tomorrow I could be in the Bahamas."

"Why the Bahamas?"

"Why not? Here, look at this book, there's any number of opportunities. You could invest – it's still classic boom time in Freeport, I could get a foothold there . . ."

She looked at him in dismay and put down the sketchpad.

"You're crazy," she said.

The phone rang. Blum picked it up. It was the tall man. If voices could sound pinched, then his was.

"We've changed our minds," he said. "We don't want the deal."

"But listen . . ."

"Read today's paper. Then you'll know why we're not interested any longer."

Click. Blum's heart lurched. Downwards.

"What is it?" asked Cora. "Good heavens, what's the matter?"

He stared at her, the receiver still in his hand.

"The bastard's called the deal off," he said after a while.

"You really scared me just then, Blum. The way you were looking at me."

He replaced the receiver. Hackensack, he thought. Maybe I'll go and see him after all.

"Well, what do you expect?" he said, lighting a cigarette. "Suppose 100 grand had just slipped through *your* fingers?"

"How do you mean? You still have the stuff. And 100,000 wasn't nearly enough. Listen, I'll keep my ears open. Perhaps something will come up."

Blum counted the last of his money. Just under DM 1,100, and the hotel bill would certainly come to more than 250. And he'd given Mr Haq 500 to no purpose. Mr Haq had made the most profit so far. He stubbed out his cigarette. His hand was trembling slightly.

"I must go out, Cora. You can keep your ears open if you like, but do be careful."

"Are we staying together, then?"

He shrugged. She got to her feet and went over to him.

"Open your mouth, Blum."

When he did, she pressed her lips to it. That full mouth. Those eyes. That long, ash-blonde hair. That warm, well-rounded body.

They agreed to meet that evening.

All Frankfurt seemed to be under the influence of cocaine. Everything was tense, all movements were jerky, awkward. Go, man, go. Finish him off. Even the layabouts were just bankers down on their luck, and the managers raced off to lunch on roller skates. Blum

112

decided not to call Hackensack first. Phone calls only meant delay. He would just go to the man's office and tackle him. Five pounds of coke, that was chemicals if you like.

On the way he went into a Tchibo coffee shop and looked through the newspapers. The dollar had recovered, excellent. So what could the tall man have meant? There it was, among the miscellaneous news items: "COFFEE AND COCAINE". On the receipt of reliable information, officers of the Special Commission of the Bavarian CID had checked up on a 28-year-old Italian in a hotel at Munich Central station and found 1.6 kilos of cocaine in his baggage, hidden in cans of coffee. It was the largest quantity ever seized in Bavaria of the South American narcotic, which had recently attained notoriety as the fashionable drug of choice. The Italian claimed to have known nothing about the cocaine in his baggage. The police suspected, said the paper, that he was a member of an international narcotics ring which intended to get a foothold in Germany.

Blum put the paper down. A hotel at Munich Central station. 1.6 kilos. The bastard. It was hard to grasp, but this time he had actually struck lucky. Cocaine in cans. 2.4 kilos of it in jumbo cans of shaving foam, 1.6 kilos in cans of Maxwell House instant coffee. Smart, but not smart enough. The cops had 1.6 kilos; Blum had the other 2.4 kilos. International narcotics ring. How does it feel, Herr Blum, to be part of an international narcotics ring? Well, gentlemen, much as you might expect in the circumstances. As always in life, it's best to remember that good things come in small cans and keep it that way. Then you'll get over the withdrawal symptoms more easily if you're left to carry the can. Stay happy on a small scale, gentlemen, because happiness is the most expensive drug of all.

21

When Blum was outside the building named on Hackensack's card as his office address he regretted not calling first. It was an old town house in the West-end area with a chestnut tree in the front garden, five storeys, a stucco façade, and Blum wonder how it could possibly accommodate all the firms, some two dozen of them, which according to the panel of doorbells had their office premises here. None of them was a Harry W. Hackensack, Consultant. He looked at the visiting card again. The address was right. Two dozen firms in the building, all sounding equally dubious. Which of them might conceal Hackensack, and why in the world should he hide his name anyway? *I've always fallen on my feet.* Company adviser nothing. All these outfits sounded like cover organizations for international drug-running and speculation rings. On the ground floor: Dr H. Mäusing, Tax Adviser, by appointment only. Dymco International. Nord–Süd Aviation. Polska Film Co. On the first floor: General Shares Fund. Letzyg Taxation Offices. Smycholsky Telecommunications. Reality Holding. Dr Immelmann, Dr Gelb, Dr von Jakubowsky, Specialists in International Law. On the second floor: Symposion. Small Businesses Institute. Taunus & Terra Films. Wurzelmayer Detective Agency. On the third floor: well, here there were six "firms", three of them under the mere abbreviations TWNF, ASE, ICA. *If I were to advise you some day you'd get a discount.* One of these must be Hackensack. Blum rang a bell. On the door hung a notice framed in brass to catch the eye and reading "NO BEGGARS OR HAWKERS". Blum did not yet feel he was a beggar, but he wasn't so sure about hawking. The door opened.

The doors on the third floor left belonged to the Trans-World Nature Fund, the Evangelical Mission to Asia and South America (Brothers of the Last Days), and the International Consulting Agency. Oh well. Blum pressed one of the three doorbells. A buzzer sounded. He opened the door and entered a musty corridor dimly lit by a 40-watt bulb. The coats on the coat-stand belonged to elderly ladies who did not care about looking chic. Some of the elderly ladies were in a large office. Blum glanced into it. They were seated tapping away at old-fashioned office typewriters, or standing in front of stacks of printed papers putting them into envelopes. There was a smell of carbon paper and dust. One of the ladies raised her head and saw Blum. Her face was as expressionless as the back of an unlicked stamp.

"What do you want?"

"I'm looking for Herr Hackensack," said Blum. "Herr Hackensack the company adviser . . ."

"Third door on the right," she said. "This is the Brothers of the Last Days Mission."

"Yes," said Blum, retreating, "so I see. Thank you very much."

The linoleum squealed. There was a small notice tacked to the third door on the right, with the information "ICA – Frankfurt" typed on it. Not very promising, thought Blum, but he knocked. He heard wooden flooring creak, and then the door was cautiously opened.

"Yes?"

A lady with a grey pageboy bob and a brown tweed

suit. Hooked nose, narrow, colourless lips, probing eyes behind glasses on a chain that hung around her neck.

"Are you the driver? You can give me the packages."

Blum assumed his professional smile.

"My name is Blum," he said. "I'm a business partner of Mr Hackensack . . . this *is* Mr Hackensack's office, isn't it?"

"This is the branch office of the International Consulting Agency," said the lady, in not unfriendly tones. Under her cool gaze, Blum began to feel less sure of himself. "Mr Hackensack isn't here at the moment."

"But can I reach him here? Maybe I could leave a message?"

The lady looked hard at Blum, at the same time inspecting his trousers. The creases in them could be made out only if you looked closely. All the same, Blum seemed to have passed muster, for she told him to come in.

The ICA office was as modest as the firm's name was grand – a scratched desk with sliding locks, a filing cabinet, an old SEL telex machine, a coat-stand with an outmoded hat and a telescopic umbrella hanging on it, hard-backed chairs, a visitor's armchair that must have come from the flea market, and on the wall, the only splash of colour, one of those tear-off calendars that pharmacists and drugstores hand out to their regular customers at Christmas. The picture for the month of March showed a bright yellow crocus. There was a door labelled "PRIVATE" in the back wall. Just enough light fell through a little window to enable you to make out, with a fair degree of certainty, whether you were reaching for the telephone receiver or the coat-stand. The window was barred. Blum wondered what there could be to steal here. Time seemed to have stood still in the ICA ever since the jazz cellar had opened and Blum had finally discovered that everything in life has its price. The tweed-clad lady sat down at the desk, but did not offer Blum a chair.

"May I ask how long you have been Mr Hackensack's business partner?"

From the way in which she said the words "business partner", Blum realized that he was on shaky ground.

"Oh, well, only since last week really. We met on Malta, and Harry – I mean Mr Hackensack – asked me to look in on him in Frankfurt. He was going to give me some business advice."

"Can you tell me what kind of business you are doing here, Mr . . .?"

"Blum. Like a flower in bloom. Well, I'm afraid that's something I'd like to discuss with Mr Hackensack personally."

"Does Mr Hackensack know?"

"Yes, of course. I just said so."

Suddenly he was sorry he hadn't snorted another line of coke before going out. The telephone rang. The lady picked it up, but said nothing. She just listened, made a note of something, and hung up.

"Well, Mr Blum, so far as I know Mr Hackensack won't be in until Monday. I'll tell him you were here, and if he thinks it's important he'll get in touch with you. Perhaps you'd leave me your card, or write down here where he can reach you . . ."

Blum lit a cigarette and blew the smoke across the desk. The lady didn't bat an eyelid. She was used to the old fellow's cigars. Typical, really, thought Blum, typical of the man to have a dump like this as his office. Carries on about power and chemicals, and now there's just the crocus on the wall and the umbrella on the coat-stand. And a mummified Prussian female at the

117

desk to scare away people like me. But I'm old enough not to be scared, mister.

"I can't be reached," he said, just a little too loud. "Just tell Mr Hackensack I was extremely sorry he wasn't able to show me Frankfurt. Frankfurt by night, of course. That's what he promised me back on Malta. Come to think of it, you can leave out the 'extremely'. Just 'sorry' will do. I'll call if I can. Goodbye."

He turned and left the office without closing the door behind him. There was a graffito carved with a knife in the lift: "Lise doesn't screw", and he thought: If I ever see him again, I must ask him the first name of the ICA's secretary.

Outside he suddenly wasn't sure why he had reacted so violently. What had he expected? A whole floor of a skyscraper gleaming with neon lights, where Hackensack and 123 employees – assisted by the latest IBM computers – laboured day and night to help people like Blum in their struggle for existence? He'd flared up like a fool. Perhaps a visit to Mr Haq was indicated. Perhaps the Pakistani had more experience in this field than he had so far admitted.

Blum took the tram, but got off again at the next stop. He hadn't been in a tram for fifteen years, and it was unnerving to be crammed among all these people and exposed to their glances. He absolutely had to have a car, but not a hire car. He mustn't sign anything. And the taxi he took cost a small fortune. That was life – talking big about investments in Freeport two hours ago, and now he had to count every coin.

This was getting to be not just hard but unfair too.

When he entered the stairway of the boarding house a ground-floor door opened, and a woman who could have been the ICA secretary's aunt stared suspiciously at him and said, "No vacancies, young man."

118

It sounded like a threat.

"I've come to visit one of your lodgers, ma'am."

"There's no one in the house."

"Mr Haq – Mr Haq from Lahore, on the third floor, he's expecting me. On business."

"On business? What kind of business, young man?"

Blum took out one of his visiting cards (Siegfried Blum – business representative – Berlin – Barcelona – Tangiers). She snatched the card from his hand, glanced at it and gave it back with a scornful grin.

"No one here to represent now. They're all gone, the whole lot of them."

"May I ask where?"

"Taken away, of course. What do you think? I always told my sister she shouldn't allow such riffraff into our place."

In the ground-floor apartment, from which a sour smell of boiled cabbage and brawn wafted, an ancient voice called: "Emmi, is that the police again? They're not to come into this house! I won't have it!"

Blum wrinkled his brow and took a step back.

"The police were here?"

"Are you hard of hearing, young man? The police, that's right, the police. I'm not letting rooms to any more Turks."

"Mr Haq is from Pakistan."

She looked at him as if he were a Pakistani himself, and a particularly unpleasant specimen. "They cooked too, that lot did, they cooked in the rooms even though I told them a hundred times not to. How am I ever to get the stink out of the furniture?"

The ancient voice called again. "No more police, Emmi, I won't have any more police here! Father would never have stood for it."

"So when were the police here?"

"They were all taken away yesterday evening, every last one of them. So what exactly were you representing for them?"

Perhaps Mr Haq had not made the most profit after all. He was certainly a clever man, and it could be that he had made off just in time. But if not . . .

Blum made his own getaway.

22

The restaurant had once been an ordinary corner café, and the low ceiling was black with smoke. You perched on uncomfortable coffee-house chairs at tiny marble-topped tables, surrounded by palm fronds, plaster statues and rubber plants, you were snubbed by waiters who had all graduated in communication aesthetics and looked like fencers or ballet dancers, and you paid twice as much for your *salade niçoise* or your *café orange* as you would anywhere else, because there was an extra attraction in the form of Art. Artistic performances were given on a platform in glaring neon lighting, by ladies who were mainly rather stout and who made silly but supposedly lascivious remarks in a voice like a carter's labourer. Blum thought, nostalgically, of Barcelona and Tangiers, of the curry nights at the Phoenicia. But of course nostalgia was out of place here. Cora was standing in the aisle on the way to the toilets, in front of the *art nouveau* posters, speaking to anyone who crossed her path. Her mouth had a rosy sheen, and she had plaited her hair into little braids. Braids, of all things. Doesn't look much like BB any more, thought Blum, but maybe that's just as well. Let's not get sentimental. When I was seventeen I wanted to be a theologian, but God couldn't care less. Now she was whispering to a repulsive character with a reddish beard who wore the dungarees that went with it. He sported the yellow badge of the anti-nuclear protesters. Badges twenty years ago had more zing to them, thought Blum.

"The way I see it, fiction's a harder drug than any-thing you can shoot up," said the man sitting beside Blum. He was tall and thin and good-looking in an unobtrusive way. Cora had introduced them, but Blum couldn't remember names. However, the man was a writer.

"Have you been shooting up already?" asked Blum, sipping his whisky.

"I meant purely metaphorically," said the man. "Your whisky there, addiction to the opposite sex, just about anything that gives us hope of realizing our true selves – they're artificial paradises. But fiction, now, that's the area where we can tread in the certainty of being bowled over by what we shall never be."

"An interesting idea," said Blum, suppressing a yawn. Cora had disappeared.

"Look at our Utopias," began the writer again, apparently inspired by having found an audience at last. "With drugs, you see, we want to experience ourselves. Sounds cheap, but it isn't. However, of course it leaves us just where we were before. But experiencing other people, and according to Sartre hell is other people – ah, that would be worth any mutilation."

"And I always thought writers led a quiet life," said Blum after a pause that threatened to go on rather too long. "Do you make a good living from your books? Are you successful?"

"As Greene said, writers are never successful."

Maybe I ought stock up on a little anthology of quotations, thought Blum. If the cops get me after all I could say: Do you know something, gentlemen? Fiction is a harder drug than anything you're about to fit me up for.

"Yes," he said finally, "that's life – hard but fair."

122

A large woman in a cloche and a feather boa minced over from the bar to the aisle. A kiss here, a greeting there. The star of the evening.

"Have you known Cora long?" asked the writer.

"Depends what you mean by long."

She had reappeared now and was talking to the star. I hope this isn't going to turn into another artists' party, thought Blum.

"And what do you think of cocaine?" he asked the writer.

"A dangerous drug," the man pontificated, drawing on his pipe. He smoked a tobacco that smelled like sheep dung. "A cynical, vain, paranoid lady, our Peruvian Lady. Remember, Hitler took pervitin daily during those last years, and you could call pervitin the number one wake-up drug."

"Really? I only know Wakey Wakey that we took during our final school exams. So carry on about cocaine."

"Maybe cocaine is the *poule de luxe* ultimately behind everything. *Cherchez la femme.*"

"Ah. And did you ever . . .?"

The writer was evasive. "Words are my drugs – the opium of nouns, the heroin of adjectives, the chemical compounds of verbs." Then, rather disdainfully: "But the authentic drugs are only useless palliatives, methods of withdrawal from fiction, like giving methadone to an addict."

Cora waved to Blum in full view of everyone. The star diseuse inspected him through a lorgnette hanging around her fat neck. Blum was annoyed. The writer leaned back and thoughtfully inspected him through the smoke.

"I had a thing with Cora once," he said at last, "but it didn't work out. Writers don't need nude models, and it got to be rather a nuisance explaining why she doesn't feature in my books." He knocked out his pipe. "Writers ought to live alone."

"And do you?" asked Blum, rising. A waiter immediately hurried over to him. He paid and mopped his brow.

"Another fiction," said the writer, opening his tobacco tin.

In the corridor, Cora put an arm around his shoulders and whispered, "Do you have two grams? Detlev's already waiting in the Gents."

Blum withdrew from her arm. "I told you it's too hot for me here. You waved to me in front of everyone – what's the idea? What do you mean, two grams? I have five pounds of the stuff, and you go on about two grams. I mean, this is ridiculous . . ."

"Every little helps," said Cora, turning back to the star diseuse.

In the Gents two men were standing at the urinal, and of course one of them was the dungaree-clad character. He pointed excitedly to the open door of the WC cubicle. The other man relieved himself, acting as if he hadn't seen anything. Blum went into the WC and slammed the door. He felt quite ill with anger. Here he was – Blum of the EC butter coup, Blum of the Titian theft – lurking around in dark toilets for customers wanting cocaine, like the last heroin hawker outside the Zoo Station. The lavatory flushed, footsteps, the rattle of the roller towel, the squealing door. Then there was a knock. Blum opened the door and was about to go out, but instead Detlev pushed his way in.

"This is safer," he whispered. He stank of garlic. His face was red; drops of sweat glistened in his red beard.

Blum took the cellophane wrapping off his cigarette packet and pressed it into his customer's hand.

"How much do you want? I don't usually sell small quantities."

"Two grams for 300, that's what I agreed with Cora."

"You're joking, son. One gram costs 250, and that's almost giving it away."

"If it's good I'll take more. I know a lot of . . ."

"Mister, I hear that ten times a day."

Someone in hobnailed boots came into the Gents and wanted to use the WC.

"Take it easy," growled Blum.

"Shit faster, can't you, mate?" said the someone, and hobnailed his way out again.

"Two grams costs 400," said Blum. "Got the money?"

"Yes, but only 300."

The smell of garlic was overpowering, but Blum stood his ground. He hadn't spent a year in the Med for nothing.

"Hand it over," he said. The red-bearded man pressed three 100-mark notes into his hand. Blum held them up to the light one by one, while his customer became increasingly nervous.

"You wouldn't be the first to try passing duds off on me," said Blum. He put the money away and brought out the pillbox in which he had put a couple of grams.

"Hold out the bag."

"Don't you have an envelope?"

"Where do you think we are, the post office?" said Blum, and began very carefully tipping the cocaine into the bag. The other man's hand was trembling so much that he spilled a little. He immediately bent and licked it off the lavatory lid. Blum, disgusted, made a face.

"Right, that's one and a half grams."

"Never! One gram at the most!"

"You'll take what you can get," said Blum, putting the pillbox away. Before going out he impressed it upon the other man, in a threatening tone, that he was not to move from the spot for five minutes. Detlev tried to object, but Blum pushed him down on the lavatory and closed the door behind him. Another one like that and I'll crack up, he thought, washing his hands. By comparison, even the porn trade was a high-society occasion.

Cora was standing at the bar, talking to a grey-haired man in an elegantly cut duffel coat. He bore a striking resemblance to Trevor Howard in *The Third Man*. Blum had last seen the film in Tangiers with Arabic subtitles. He nodded to the man and said to Cora, "Come on, let's get out of here."

"This is James," said Cora. James's expression was neutral, and he looked at Blum in silence as if waiting for an explanation. But Blum had nothing to explain.

"See you later, then," he told Cora, and made his way past the marble-topped tables and the wasp-waisted waiters and the palm fronds and the women with their raucous voices. The writer was still sitting in the same place, smoking his pipe. A girl who was at the most half his age was talking to him. Him and his fictions, thought Blum, but he wished the writer luck. The star was now standing on the platform with a top hat on her green wig. She announced, imperiously:

> "Night is not the time for sleep,
> Night will chase away ennui.
> A ship leaves harbour for the deep,
> The vessel must put out to sea . . ."

Outside, Blum was vainly looking for a taxi when Cora appeared beside him. She took his arm. With her boots on she was as tall as him.

"What's the matter, Blum? What have I done wrong?"

"If you bring me another like that Detlev . . ."

"He's no worse than anyone else."

"Are all these characters really your friends?"

"What do you mean?"

"Well, that writer, for instance."

"Oh, him. All he can do is talk."

"Where did you live together? In Munich?"

"Who cares? Is that what he said? Talk about boastful!"

"And this man James . . ."

"Heavens, you really don't need to be jealous of him. I know him professionally. He's a fantastic fashion photographer, but now he's retired. All he photographs is frogs."

"Ah. I understand. So you were a model?"

"You don't understand anything. What are you really doing here?"

"Trying to sell five pounds of cocaine. And you bring me a stinker like that Detlev with his stinking 300 marks in his dungarees. How a grown man can choose to wear dungarees . . ."

"You think you look more like a grown man with that cravat of yours? I thought you urgently needed money. Aren't 300 marks money? I've been known to work a week for that much."

"Yes, well. Just fancy. I tell you, another three days of scraping about like this and I'll be in jail. And the anti-nuclear demonstrators won't be getting me out."

"Oh, come off it. There's so much going on here no one will notice you. Don't take everything so seriously. Anyway, I've made a date for twelve-thirty with a character who wants a whole fifteen grams. That's something, right?"

"Fifteen grams for how much?"

"Three thousand, I said."

"Good heavens, with fifteen grams you start by asking 4,000. I mean, these guys are rolling in money. You could ask 5,000. When I think of Morocco . . ."

"Oh, ask what you like. It's your coke. I wish I knew why I'm helping you."

"Because you want a slice of the pie too."

"You really think that?"

They stared at each other.

"Of course I think so. It may not be the only thing I'm thinking."

Her full lips pouted, then she laughed and took his arm again.

"Come on, let's earn that 3,000 and then get out. I'm sick and tired of Frankfurt."

"How long have you been here?"

"Far too long, Blum."

"And where do you want to go?"

"Amsterdam, maybe. Come with me. You'll get rid of the stuff much more easily there."

"I'll have to put a bit more money into the operation first, or it'll all fall through."

At last a taxi stopped.

23

Blum took the notes out of his pocket and smoothed them flat – a good feeling. Three red notes, seventeen blue notes, assorted small change, the kilos, the pounds of cocaine.

"You should see yourself," said Cora, lying in the armchair and fiddling with the radio. "You look like you were in church."

"Money is life, baby. And life is sacred, right?"

"Don't keep calling me baby. I hate it."

"What did that pimp say to you?"

"What pimp?"

"Don't pretend you didn't know the character who bought those fifteen grams is a pimp."

"Toni? You're crazy. He works in a publishing firm."

"Oh yes, in a publishing firm? So why did he tell me he needed the stuff for his chicks?"

She laughed. She was wearing only her shirt and the dirty silver cowboy boots. She had rolled up her ringlets again and pinned her hair up.

"That's just talk, Blum. He probably means his books."

"Oh. And that James has a thing about frogs. Does he mean cornflakes?"

"Cornflakes?"

"That's right, cornflakes. Peruvian cornflakes. You know who he reminds me of? Trevor Howard in *The Third Man*?"

"Trevor Howard?"

"Never heard of him? No idea about *The Third Man*? How you manage to get through life at all is a mystery to me."

"You don't make a very attractive grandpa, Blum."

He stowed the money away in his wallet with his visiting cards, snapshots and hotel bills. Three thousand, ridiculous. He'd hoped to finish the day with 100 grand. So good things came in small cans – more like tiny ones. Happiness was playing hard to get.

"What did you say?" he asked abstractedly. He tidied up his things; it was a ritual. His ankleboots needed cleaning again too, he thought. Why wasn't there any shoe polish here?

"I said you needn't carry on as if you were my grandpa. Hey, are you asleep?"

She listened to a few bars of Beethoven and then went on fiddling with the radio. Blum frowned. Not the right moment for his ritual. He lit a cigarette and lay down on the bed. Fully clothed.

"Why do you smoke HB?"

"HB?"

"Yes, your cigarette brand."

"My dear child, I've been smoking them since I was fourteen. HB was the first filter cigarette."

"I don't believe you."

"The first I liked. I never smoke anything else."

"You think there'll be HB in the Bahamas?"

This did not merit an answer. He blew a smoke ring instead. It worked the second time. Perfect.

"What's that? Listen."

She had switched over to short-wave and found the female voice broadcasting its code into the night, that mysterious litany of figures:

"79 576 – 00 253 – 72 187 – 11 334 – 30 362 – 70 679 – 07 387 – "

Each set of figures was repeated. Tonight the voice had a slight Saxon accent.

"What's that?"

"You can hear."

"But what does it mean?"

"It's for agents."

"Agents?"

"Yup, agents. We live in a world full of agents, Cora. Didn't you know?"

"I had an agent when I was modelling."

"Not that sort of agent. Real ones."

"So what do they do?"

"What we all do – they collect information and pass it on. Only they're pros."

"You mean spies?"

"Spies too."

"But you're not a spy."

"That depends. I'm on the *qui vive* as well. How would I have come by the coke if I hadn't checked things out?"

"It was coincidence, Blum."

"There's no such thing as coincidence in this line of business. Come to bed."

"So you think we're agents? Me too?"

"No, of course not you too. You're the kind who breaks all the moulds."

"You honestly think they're passing news on to agents over the radio?"

"Of course."

"Who are *they*, then?"

"Doesn't matter. Them, us, everyone. Everyone's doing it. Information is power. Take my five pounds of coke, for instance. Anyone who knows about it has information that's worth a lot to certain people. Understand?"

"You still don't trust me."

"Oh yes, I trust you. Up to a point. But if the CID pick you up and promise you immunity from prosecution, you'll give me away."

"I wouldn't give you away, Blum."

"Why not? Because I'm such a handsome guy? Don't kid yourself, girlie. Deception rules the world, and betrayal is its elder brother."

"But how can you live with that? How can you live in a world made up entirely of deception and betrayal and agents and fear and cops and money and theft and murder and spies and power?"

He stubbed his cigarette out and picked up his tooth-glass of whisky.

"That's all I've ever learned about," he said.

"But it can't be right!" She was savaging the armchair with the heels of her boots. "That's not the world we live in."

"What is, then?"

She looked at him, shaking her head. Then she said quietly, "You're beginning to get to me, you and your fears."

"There's no need for you to be afraid. You only have to walk out of the door, and then you just have to shut your eyes tight and act as if —"

"I'm afraid of something happening to you."

"*You're* afraid of something happening to *me?*"

"Not jail or that. Something much worse."

"Something worse than jail?

"Yes. Why not just throw away the key and forget about the stuff?"

"You're telling me to throw away the key? The key to the left-luggage locker? The key to 100 grand? The key to Freeport, Bahamas? To my next two or three years?"

"You can live on something else. You said so yourself, you always get by. But with this stuff – it doesn't have to be like that. This fear – it's not worth wearing yourself down over it."

"If I had to make a living selling shoelaces maybe I wouldn't be so scared. But I can tell you one thing: my fear of having to make a living selling shoelaces is much greater than my fear of a couple of drugs syndicates or a few years in jail."

"I thought nothing could be worse than jail?"

"The worst part is not being able to take any more risks. Everyone has one leg in jail all his life, you might say. But the other leg has to be able to go the full distance. What would I get if they caught me? Six years, maybe. In practice four. The money's worth it."

"Blum, that doesn't make sense. No kind of money is worth it. Money's not really worth anything"

"It's all very well for you to say so. You haven't known times when people would queue all day for a half-rotten cabbage."

"What's that got to do with it?"

"Nothing, Cora. And everything."

She took her boots off, stood up, went over to the bed and lay down with him.

"Listen, I know two Germans in Amsterdam. They've been living there a long time, they know their way around. They're really clever businessmen, and they deal in dope too. You could sell the coke to them straight off. Let's just go to Amsterdam."

She began unbuttoning his shirt. Her long hair brushed his chest.

"If you know all that . . . maybe you know someone else here, right? I wouldn't mind having more than a couple of grand in my pocket before making for Amsterdam."

She undid his belt and massaged his stomach.

"I do know someone. Not right here in town, in the country. He'd be sure to buy 50 or 100 grams."

Blum managed to summon up a remnant of distrust.

"Do I know this person?"

"No," she said, pulling his trousers down. *Mamma mia*, thought Blum later, what a woman, curvaceous and juicy and skilful and loveable, except that she never says a thing about herself. Was this the high point of happiness? But later still, in the night, he realized how much he too was keeping back, and when they lay side by side in the dark, in silence, it seemed to him as if they were further apart from each other than they had been close before.

24

Cora had rustled up a car from somewhere, a battered Beetle painted all over by a previous owner with flowers, suns and stars and moons and angels that were now being eaten away by rust.

"You want me to drive a thing like that?" asked Blum incredulously, when she picked him up from the hotel in it.

"You don't have to do the driving," she replied coolly, and nor did he – she steered the car skilfully through the traffic jams of Frankfurt and out into the country. The sun was even shining, a cold and slightly rusty sun that suited this concrete desert.

"Ghastly, isn't it?"

"Depends how you see it. I don't think the people here would be happy to swap places with Mr Haq, though I bet you can eat better in Pakistan."

She laughed.

"Aren't you going to tell me where we're going?"

"Let's make it a surprise for you."

"With 100 grams of cocaine in my pocket I'm not too keen on surprises."

"Let's say it's a nice surprise."

The housing estates were fewer and farther between now; they were driving through open country. Old snow lay everywhere, and flocks of crows flew over the dark forests of fir trees. Blum shivered, although the heating in this old banger actually worked.

"You seem to know your way around. Have you lived in Frankfurt long?"

She wasn't to be drawn out. "What are you really planning to do with the money, Blum? You can't be serious about investments in the Bahamas."

He sensed that the question really mattered to her. Lighting a cigarette, he looked out at the frozen countryside.

"Some day I'd like to live on a little island with a few friends. It doesn't have to be in the Bahamas. Maybe I'd run a bar, nothing too smart, a nice cool little place down by the harbour where you could see the boats through the window. Perhaps a few chairs outside under an awning, for tourists. A dish of the day, otherwise just sandwiches and drinks, but the best available. You could go fishing, visit the casino on the neighbouring island now and then. Everyone could do as they liked. Once a week I'd go to the brothel with the vice-consul and the English novelist and the liquor smuggler, to hear all the stories. I know you don't like stories, but maybe you don't need them. Memories are crap, but stories hold life together. Sometimes, when you have the horrors, only a good story will help."

After a while she asked: "Could I come and live on your island?"

"It wouldn't be *my* island, Cora."

"Your bar, though."

"Yes, it would be my bar."

"Could I visit your bar?"

"So long as you didn't make a fuss. The fuss that women can make – well, that's another story."

"You know I don't like stories."

"I wouldn't forbid you the place, not straight away," said Blum smiling, and stubbed out his cigarette.

136

"I like you, Blum," she said quietly, staring ahead at the straight, empty road.

"I like you too," he murmured. It was a long time since a woman had last told him she liked him – the tourists and whores didn't count – but now he sat silent in the rickety car, and in the silence he felt confusion and suspicion growing in him. Was Cora like the tourists, was she a whore too? Or was he so poisoned by suspicion that he could see nothing but calculation even in such words? They drove on, still in silence.

Finally Cora turned off the road where a path ran across the fields and parked the car outside a garden run wild. He saw the metallic gleam of a Mercedes 450. There was a white bungalow in the garden, and further away, on the outskirts of the woods, an old farmhouse. Smoke curled from its chimney. Blum recognized the man who came to the bungalow door as they walked through the garden. This time he was wearing a Shetland pullover instead of a duffel coat, but with his beret, his grey moustache and his jutting chin he could still have been Trevor Howard as Major Calloway, or at least Trevor Howard's double.

25

"What'll you drink – sherry, port, gin? Or would you like to try the local cider?"

"I'd like a beer if you have one."

"Of course. Will you see to it, Margot?"

Margot saw to it. She was somewhere in her mid-twenties, an ethereal dark-haired beauty beside whom Cora was a figure in the purest rustic Baroque manner. The bungalow was well furnished, its rural style relieved by a good deal of glass and technological devices. The rugs alone were worth a fortune, Blum estimated, and among the pictures he spotted a Corot which wasn't necessarily a forgery. You could see the back garden and the dilapidated-looking farmhouse through the glass wall of windows. A log fire crackled on the hearth. Not a bad life for a retired fashion photographer.

Margot brought the beer. Heineken. The master of the house drank a sherry, the women said they didn't want anything. Instead, they kept a conversation going. After a while Margot said she wanted to show Cora something, and they went into the next room

"The girls are old friends," said James, raising his glass to Blum.

"Cora says you're only photographing frogs these days?"

James smiled as ironically as Major Calloway in the film when he is discussing Westerns with the writer Holly Martins. Not that Blum was any Joseph Cotten.

"Frogs will soon be extinct, did you know that, Blum?" He put another log of wood on the fire. Then he sat down in a leather armchair, crossed his legs in their white jeans, and said: "So you're in the cocaine business?" What was it Calloway had said to Martins? "I didn't know there were tigers in Arizona."

Blum said something about a good opportunity. You took things as they came. These days you had to be adaptable. If something would make a profit you couldn't hold back like a gentleman, those days were past. And who went about all day with a copy of the narcotics laws in his pocket?

Not James for one. "I have certain reasons for taking an interest in cocaine," he said.

"I can imagine. You feed it to the frogs, do you?"

"Yes, Cora mentioned your sense of humour. Don't you take it yourself?"

"I could develop a taste for it. Particularly with the stuff I have at the moment. Genuinely first class. Amazing what one can yet discover."

"How do you mean?"

"At twenty I discovered a taste for sex, at thirty for whisky and now for cocaine. Where will it all end?"

"I'd say you were going onwards and upwards. May I try it?"

Blum handed him the pillbox. James took a pure gold cocaine set from the secret drawer of his desk and sniffed the snow through a ten-pound note. Bank of England notes, he said, were best for the purpose – only notes from the old series, though; the paper of the new ones wasn't as good. Blum allowed himself a pinch too. The stuff flew up his nostrils as if of its own accord. He had not stinted, and the effect of the cocaine took his breath away for a moment. Carefully, he lit a cigarette. It did not explode. He slowly returned to his flesh and blood body, but his mind was still high in the air above the valleys. Ice sparkled in the sun on the glaciers.

"Very clean," said James, who was resurfacing too. "Hardly cut with anything."

"Hardly? Not at all! Straight from the producer."

"Really? Did you buy it there yourself?"

"Not exactly, but the people I got it from are 100 per cent reliable. They buy only the very best of the best. This stuff comes straight from the Andes. Peruvian flake, if you know what that means."

"And how much do you have for sale?"

Blum flicked a mote of dust off his sleeve. He saw Cora and Margot walking up and down the garden, with a Dalmatian running around among the hedges.

"You can have enough," he said. "The question is, can you afford it? This stuff is bloody expensive."

There was a superior smile on James's face. Calloway, with his major's salary, couldn't have afforded that smile.

"Within reason, I can pay any price. You see, I'm buying for various acquaintances who don't want to feature personally in any deal. All of them people at the very top – of industry, the press, art, politics."

"Politics?"

"How do you think politicians can stand the job? Wine tastings and beer festivals aren't always enough for them."

"I thought only Hitler needed this kind of thing."

"Hitler was an eccentric. Today cocaine is a status symbol, and the more stylish politicians would like to be in on the act. I myself, of course, am entirely non-political, but it can sometimes be useful to have such connections."

"Naturally," said Blum. "Of course, that doesn't exactly lower the price."

"Politicians don't earn much, my dear fellow."

"No one believes that these days, not even people at beer festivals," said Blum. He was enjoying this conversation. Things were definitely looking up.

"What would you want for 100 grams?"

"Only 100 grams? Why not take a pound? Then I can give you something in the nature of a discount for quantity."

But James played it down. He stroked his moustache as if to ensure that every single hair was in place – perhaps he had given up smoking and now didn't know what to do with his fingers – and frowned heavily. Later, perhaps, he said; he was sure they would keep in touch. As he spoke his eyes wandered over the figures in the garden.

"A hundred grams would do for a start. Of course, I shall have to find out if we can come up with the money in a hurry . . ."

Blum's hand holding the beer glass was suspended in mid-air. "What do you mean?"

"Well, I don't suppose you'd be particularly happy with a cheque. So we must get the cash together."

Blum put the glass down on the table without drinking from it. "Why do you all have such trouble finding cash? Everyone keeps saying cash is in short supply, cash is difficult, cash is a problem. And yet you're all rolling in money."

"You yourself, as a businessman . . ."

"Oh, never mind the soft soap! You just see me as a miserable rat of a dealer to be strung along until you can pull a fast one on me —"

"I don't see why you're so agitated —"

But there was no holding Blum now. All his anger and pent-up fears insisted on breaking out at last. He could understand wretched addicts having difficulty getting the dough together, he said, but they'd do it and pay cash down, even if it was all in small change. As for the smart alecs in the arts and crafts line, he was fed up to the teeth with them. And if politicians were going to plead cash-flow problems, they'd better buy their stuff by the gram on the open market. Or next time they went on some foreign development aid trip . . .

"If you have two days to spare," James finally said, soothingly, "of course you can have your cash."

"But I don't have two days to spare. Didn't Cora tell you? You're forgetting that I'm running all the risk in this business."

"I've been buying cocaine for years, and I've never yet heard of one of the big dealers being busted. Suppliers maybe, yes. They picked one up in Munich the day before yesterday. You'll have heard about it. I hope it wasn't your man. But dealers really are very seldom busted . . ."

"It wasn't my man. You think I'd be stupid enough to have the stuff packed in coffee cans?"

James did not think so. He took another small pinch.

"Get me political protection," said Blum, tapping out the rhythm of his remarks with a cigarette, "and I'll accept any kind of payment – even in stocks and shares."

"You don't mean that seriously."

"I do."

"We're not living in some banana republic, for heaven's sake. Political protection, give me patience! Your own stuff has gone to your head."

Blum lit his cigarette and blew the smoke in James's face.

"As I said, I keep well out of it."

142

"But you're right in the middle of it, my dear fellow. Let me tell you something, right now I'm getting myself political protection from the USA. You don't believe me? Then call this number. An office in Frankfurt. The ICA. Obviously it's a cover organization. Ask for a Mr Hackensack. Harry W. Hackensack. My friend Harry. Of course that's not his real name, but Hackensack will do. Go on, call him. He'll tell you. Banana republic? You must be joking."

James wore a rather pained expression. He really must have learned it from Trevor Howard.

"I'll do no such thing, Blum. We had better agree on the price now. I really am not particularly interested in the details of your trade."

"I knew it – the way you see it I'm only a supplier, I'm inferior." Just in time, Blum noticed the changed expression in his customer's eyes, and put the brakes on. After all, he was not a frog. Then James smiled his impersonal smile again.

"How much do you want for 100 grams, then?"

"Fifteen grand."

"That's a lot of money."

"It's a lot of cocaine too."

"And you'd have to give some kind of discount for payment in cash."

"You're not going to haggle over a stupid few hundred marks?"

"I was thinking of a couple of grams."

"Okay, I don't mind splashing out – I'll leave you the pillbox. There's at least six grams in there."

James nodded, and rose rather stiffly from his armchair. "Then I'll go and phone the interested parties."

"I don't have much time, mister," Blum warned him.

"I thought time was of the essence in your profession. The beer's in the kitchen."

Blum got himself another. He drank it slowly, watching the sun sink behind the fir trees, as Cora and Margot disappeared into the farmhouse. *I like you, Blum.* What did she mean by that? She might as well have said: I like my steak well done. He knew that was not so, but he couldn't keep back the thought. Such vague language blurred everything. You knew where you were with whores and tourists. A pair of shoes for Fatima of the Kasbah, a torrid holiday romance for the hairdresser from Hameln. I like you, that sounded definite enough, but all it meant was: now we're quits. But why did Cora want to be quits with him?

When he had drunk his beer James came back and said everything was going smoothly. "You'll get your money this evening."

Blum looked at his watch. It was twenty past five. "What do you mean by this evening?"

"Patience, Blum, patience. A couple of hours – maybe eleven or twelve o'clock. There's all you need here – Margot can cook a meal, there's plenty to drink in the house, you can read or go for a walk or watch TV, and if you want to go to bed there are plenty of rooms over in the farmhouse. The people who live there are understanding folk, you won't be in their way."

"The people who live there?"

"I let a few people who've had certain difficulties in town stay there."

"That's very nice of you, James, but I don't know if I can hang around that long. We really wanted to leave for Amsterdam this evening."

"You're buying in Amsterdam?"

"Edam cheese, yes."

They stared at each other. James forced himself to make a casual gesture. "Have a drink, Blum. Scotch?"

He drank J&B. Where else had he drunk J&B recently? With Hermes. Hermes and James. There must be a link. J&H. The ex-photographer and the ex-dealer. Frogs and daughters. Blum helped himself to another Scotch, but added plenty of soda. He wandered around the big room, looked at the pictures, and in a corner, under two crossed Turkish sabres, found a slate slab on which someone had written in chalk: "At ten man becomes an animal, at twenty a madman, at thirty a failure, at forty a swindler and at fifty a criminal."

"Who wrote that?" he asked James, who was putting a book back on the shelves.

"A Japanese poet. I found it in Henry Miller. How old are you, Blum?"

"Thirty-nine," said Blum.

"There, you see? And I'm forty-nine"

26

It was cold outside. The last of the daylight was fading behind the woods. Mist over the meadows, crows on the branches of the fruit trees. Blum swore as his ankleboots sank into the muddy ground. Bloody shit, bloody filth, bloody crazy. Five pounds of coke and still no land in sight.

A rotting kitchen garden lay in front of the farmhouse. Weeds rambled over rusty tin cans. Scraps of a woman's blouse hung on a dead tomato plant leaning sideways. From the house – its roof was covered with moss – he heard loud metallic clanging, groaning, some kind of singsong. Carefully, Blum made his way up the slippery steps and opened the door.

The clanging and singing came from a room on his right. The door to the room was not locked, and Blum slowly opened it. The noise drowned the squeal of the rusty hinges. They were squatting on a pile of old mattresses in a big, smoky, unheated room, muffled up in sweaters, jackets, blankets and curtains, about a dozen men and women all with the same long hair and pale faces, drumming on baking tins, saucepans, fuel canisters and tar barrels, bawling out their song to the sound. It was like the party in Munich all over again:

"Awawawa-ah!"

"Ululululu-uh!"

"Awawawawa-ah!"

"Ululululululu-uh!"

Candles and incense sticks were burning here too, and one man was stripping in front of the company; there was no snake coiled around his torso, but a whip-lash that he was using to strike himself in time with the jungle sounds. His shadow danced over the wall, where the plaster was flaking away. Blum closed the door again, turned and opened the door opposite. This was the kitchen. In contrast to the exterior of the house it was comfortable, clean and warm. There was even a fridge, and a kitten purring in front of a saucer of milk. Two young men in dark caftans were sitting on a window-seat in the corner in front of the remains of a meal. One was reading out figures from a sheet of paper while the other fed them into a pocket calculator.

"Comes to 456,787.92," he said.

"Deutschmarks or dollars?" asked Blum.

They gave him no more than a fleeting glance. "Meetings only on Sundays," said the man with the calculator, and went on with his sums. Blum thanked him for the information and closed the door. Suddenly he realized that his nerves were stretched to breaking point. Cold sweat stood out on his forehead. His hand trembled as it held his lighter to a cigarette. The next door was ajar too, and before Blum opened it he heard Cora's voice. His hand slowly withdrew.

"I haven't told him," said Cora.

"I wouldn't either if I were you." That was Margot.

"But that wouldn't be fair. I mean, I owe him something."

"Suppose you do tell him. You can't know how he'll react."

"Oh, he's too old to rant and rave or anything."

"But if you simply go on this way . . ."

That was enough for Blum. He didn't want to know any more. Perhaps he really was too old to rant and rave, but he was certainly not too old to realize what was going on. He'd been right; he ought to have relied on his instinct from the first. They'd planted her on him. Of course they knew he liked her type. Your tastes were no secret by the time you were forty. And now she was wondering whether to come clean. The classic case – she'd fallen for him. It might sound improbable, but the most improbable answer was always the right one. The more improbable the more likely to be right. And where there was money involved it was always safe to assume that everyone was out to cheat you. He quietly left the house and went back to the bungalow. Deception and betrayal, betrayal and deception, brothers down the ages. James was sitting in his armchair, putting a film into a camera. The Dalmatian beside him growled.

"It's okay, Orlando. This is Herr Blum, our new cocaine dealer. Kind of looks as if he doesn't like you, Blum."

"Too bad for him. Who was your old dealer, then? Hermes?"

James frowned. So I was right, thought Blum. He wondered if he'd reach the VW if James set the dog on him. He had no experience of fighting off savage dogs with a flick-knife. But the dog didn't look savage. He too was only a double, like his master. Blum supposed he'd just have to write off the six grams in the pillbox.

"Ah, you mean Hermes in Munich," said James. "But he retired ages ago. Isn't he breeding horses now?"

"Daughters," said Blum.

"That's right, he never could keep his hands off the girls. How odd that you know him too."

"We're colleagues, after all," said Blum. "Not that a little thing like that counts in this line of trade."

James passed his hand over his beret and looked hard at Blum.

"What do you mean? Sit down, Blum. You make me quite nervous standing there like that."

"You know what I mean. You can tell Hermes from me, thanks but no thanks. If he wants the stuff he'll have to see about it for himself."

He ran across the garden, the knife in his right hand, and flung open the door of the VW with his left. Then he saw that Cora had taken the key out. It had still been in the ignition when she parked. He didn't even think of trying the Mercedes. He simply ran on through the slush and mud. It was dark now. Behind him he heard James calling and the dog barking, but no one was following him. He had taken them by surprise. It was always an advantage to be a little quicker off the mark than other people. Gasping, he reached the road, ran down the slope and disappeared into the woods.

27

The breakfast room was also available to guests as a TV room in the evenings. Blum had it to himself. He chose the most comfortable chair and placed another in front of it so that he could put his feet up, and stood yet another chair beside it for his beer, his hamburger and the ashtray. The last two hours were among the worst Blum could remember, and he had known some really bad ones. By comparison, waiting around at Malta airport had been the purest South Seas holiday. First the woods, the darkness and the animals, then two miles along the road when no one would stop to give him a lift, then three-quarters of an hour in the bar attached to the gym in the nearest village waiting for a taxi that had to come out from the local town. You could have four lines of coke inside you in a big city, even on the tram, even in the local government offices, even at a meeting of members of the police sports club – fine, no problem. But a head full of snow in the bar next to the gym of some dump in the Taunus, on a Friday evening before the bowling begins – no thanks. Or not, anyway, after an hour in the woods and on the road, wearing Spanish ankleboots meant for an evening stroll down the avenidas, with your trousers stiff with mud up to the calves, fir needles and birdshit on your jacket, and an icy chill in your limbs that was outdone only by the hatred he felt for Cora. And the taxi ride had been no picnic either, what with the driver's endless chatter, the fear that the man would simply drop him off at the nearest police station – "Got to be a sex murderer for sure, sergeant, comes straight out of the woods, and he's not from hereabouts" – and the certainty that by now Cora had been in his room long ago, and the key to the left-luggage locker was gone for ever.

He bit a piece off his hamburger, drank some beer and switched on the TV. What did the world have to offer? At least the key had still been in place under the bedside table, untouched, where he had moved it, the hair he had left as a precaution still on the sticky tape. The game went on.

He had taken another bite when he suddenly saw Mr Haq on the screen. No doubt about it – there he stood, surrounded by his fellow countrymen and uniformed police, on an airport concourse, smiling straight at the camera. He was wearing his green suit and black tie. The colours showed up well. Blum found the volume control.

". . . the first group of illegal immigrants to be deported to their home countries by the state of Hesse. The Interior Ministry has established that they came to the Federal Republic for purely economic reasons. Most are from Pakistan and travelled by way of East Berlin. The influx of asylum seekers continues. We will now hear what the Frankfurt City Council has to say. Over to our reporter on the crisis team in the Römer building . . ."

Mr Haq raised his hand, waved, and then made Winston Churchill's famous V for Victory sign. He's telling me that we'll win through, thought Blum. Clever fellow. A professional making his mark. Blum switched over to another channel. So Mr Haq had been deported. Tomorrow he could be eating with his wife again. Perhaps Jeddah would have been better after all. Blum threw the rest of his hamburger into the wastepaper basket. All that good curry. Billiards at the Punjab Club. Daughters. How far would DM 500 go in Lahore? Not far enough for a comfortable retirement, for sure. But perhaps Mr Haq had made most profit after all. At least he was home again.

"I think there's something on Two," said a man whose presence Blum hadn't even noticed. Had he been sitting here all the time? No, impossible. He was just opening a beer. A tall, sturdy fellow in a badly fitting blue suit worn with a red jersey shirt. Kindly face. Blum switched over to Channel Two. The man sat behind and to one side of him. The programme he wanted was called *File XY – Case Still Open*. The presenter was just greeting studio guests in Vienna, Zurich and Munich. As Blum didn't know the series it took him a moment to realize that the studio guests were CID officers, particularly as the detective-superintendent in Munich was a smart young woman. So now he was going to get a survey of the activities of the German-speaking criminal fraternity. Not that East Germany was included, very likely there *was* no German-speaking criminal fraternity there. And Mr Haq was in his plane flying east. Maybe they'd stop over in Bahrain and he'd succeed in bribing a Bahraini official and going underground. It wasn't all that far from Bahrain to Jeddah. Hm. That's life: hard, but sometimes fair. At least mosquitoes don't live as long.

The man behind Blum cleared his throat, but when Blum turned round he simply gave a foolish grin and raised his beer bottle. Blum nodded, drank too, and turned back to the film. Or rather it was not a film but real life, or anyway an imitation of real life, so a film after all. A search was going on in the Cologne area for the murderer of a police officer. A large-scale manhunt.

"The search is in full swing." A DM 9,000 reward. So a human being was worth less than a bag of cocaine. But cocaine was power. Hermes had planted her on him, and then her conscience pricked her. Blum was beginning to feel queasy. The effects of the cocaine in his head were subsiding, and the sense of being on a high, still in charge in spite of everything, was evaporating. The TV room looked really dreary, and from the street came the usual raucous noise and cowboy music from the American joint on the corner. What a miserable neighbourhood. One of the wanted men would have looked like Blum if his hair had been darker, and he imagined himself already on TV, the subject of a manhunt.

"The wanted man", the presenter would say with suitable solemnity, "has no previous convictions, but is notable for considerable criminal energy and does not shrink from threats of violence. He is the kind of character who was frequently found in the 1970s: an educated man who has failed to make his mark in a respectable career. Such people are particularly apt to become involved in economic crime, pornography and the drugs trade. After several unsuccesful attempts to gain a footing in an honest way of life, the man, who briefly attained some fame in certain circles as 'Buttercup Blum', had gone to ground abroad, where he obviously made contact with international narcotics rings. On returning to the Federal Republic he immediately became involved in the drugs scene. He is probably under the influence of the fashionable drug cocaine, which has recently attained unfortunate prominence, and we must assume that he is armed. I will now go over to Detective-Superintendent Hackensack of the Frankfurt Special Commission for a situation report . . ."

Blum mopped the sweat from his brow. Suddenly he thought he smelled the sour breath of the man behind him. An intrusive character. God knew why the man wanted to watch a TV show like this. Maybe he himself was a small-time crook gaping at the big boys. Blum reached for his beer. Lukewarm. He had stomach cramps. It was time to beat a retreat, return to a well-ordered life. After Cora, only strategic thinking would do any good. Even the frogs only *seemed* to be croaking away in the swamps without a care in the world. The real fact was that everyone had an ulterior plan.

"Don't you like it?" asked the big man in tones of concern. "I just thought a bit of excitement wouldn't hurt."

"I've had enough excitement for one day, thanks," said Blum. At this moment the door opened and another TV fan entered the room.

The second man was a Mediterranean type – small, wiry, with black hair and curly mutton-chop whiskers at the sides of his face. He was wearing a pale blue silk suit with a waistcoat, and a red-spotted white cravat with a gold pin. The rings on his fingers must weigh a full ounce of gold. He was smoking a cigarette in a black holder. Through the thick lenses of his glasses, his eyes looked like those of a deep-sea fish in an aquarium. They were toad's eyes, moray eel's eyes, the eyes of a killer frog. He was smiling extravagantly.

"I 'ope I no disturb? Sit down, sit down, *mein 'err*! German televisione *benissimo*."

He nodded briefly to the other man and simply pushed Blum back down in his chair. Then he sat down by the door. Blum forced himself to keep calm. They'd got him. Never mind who they were. Rossi, the "other side", it made no difference. If they'd wanted to kill him they'd have done it by now. So they were just keeping him here until the others had searched his room at their leisure and found the key. Now he remembered the funny way the porter had looked at him. It wasn't the state of his suit. No, it was the instructions he'd had from the leader of the gang. Too bad for Hermes, who must certainly be on his way too. Blum's thoughts became muddled, clashed, came up against the gratings being let down all over his mind because it was closing time in the store. If only he'd done the deal with James. Fifteen grand wouldn't have been a bad way to conclude it. Expecting half a million was crazy anyway. A hundred grand, that might have come off, that was within the realms of possibility, he'd almost been there before in the past. But in view of his run of bad luck over these last few years, even fifteen grand wouldn't have been too bad. Just enough for him to go underground somewhere, wait till all this had blown over and then start again somewhere else. With fifteen grand you wouldn't have to wash glasses in the Punjab Club, and the boom in Freeport was more of a fairy-tale told for losers anyway. Fifteen grand would have done nicely. A good round little sum. But then James knew Hermes . . . Cora and Hermes . . . Hermes and Henri – no, that would never have worked either. *The cocaine trade is something of a closed shop.* Not for amateurs, and if amateurs did try they'd be shown where the line was drawn.

A sex murder had been committed in Zurich, and Frankfurt announced the theft of bars of silver to the value of DM 1.1 million. The reward for information leading to the arrest of the thief and the recovery of the silver was DM 110,000, "the 10 per cent usual in such cases". So a good tip was worth almost more than five pounds of coke.

The Italian clicked his tongue and offered Blum a cigarette. Didn't people on death row get a final cigarette before the execution? Were they going to stuff a toad down his throat next, or what exactly did the syndicate do to people who meddled in their business? He'd blame it all on Rossi, and rightly so, of course – Rossi had given him the left-luggage receipt, and then there were the strikes in Italy – no connection – shaving foam, *capisco?* – *Madonna salvani.* But probably Rossi was turning his room inside out at this very moment. Blum gave the Italian a light. His hand was perfectly steady, although he noticed both the men looking at him.

"Good cigarette. What brand is it?"

"*Sigaretta arabica.* Cairo."

"Ah, Egypt. Oriental tobacco. Tastes like it."

"*Si.*"

There was nothing for it, Blum had to go on watching the *XY* programme. If he kept calm surely he'd be all right. Suddenly he felt the plastic bag containing the 100 grams he'd been carrying around with him all day. Cora had spoken of 100 grams. James too. Remarkable how ridiculous their little agreements were. But the 100 grams were still in his right inside pocket, where he usually kept his wallet. Blum was clever, he didn't put his wallet in his left inside pocket, like all other right-handers. A hundred grams, that would be twenty grand if he went about it the right way. The picture on screen was flickering before his eyes, but he forced himself to listen. They were wondering why the murderer of the policeman, still on the loose despite a major manhunt, had shot the officer. He had no previous form except for breaking and entering.

"He must somehow have gone off the rails," the superintendent was saying.

156

"That's very illuminating," replied the presenter. Outside, the sirens howled. Trains often got derailed at night. It was only from the reaction of his two guards – for by now they had openly stationed themselves one on each side of him, beer bottles between them, a cosy Father's Day picture – that Blum realized something was wrong. From down below in the hotel lobby came noise, agitated voices, the banging of doors. The Italian glanced at the German. He rose and opened the door a crack. A woman's indignant protests could now be clearly heard – it must be the manageress – and above a babble of voices there suddenly came the sound of a fist hammering on a door, and the unmistakable words: "Open up there! Police!"

Next moment both Blum's guards were out of the door and on the stairs, but they were already being restrained by two men in leather jackets. Passport control. A *razzia*. Terrorism. Blum had to get a grip on himself so as not to break into crazy laughter.

"Your ID, please."

The policeman was wearing a blue raincoat and had a weary face. The corners of his mouth showed the malice of which he was capable. Inspector Cassar had looked quite different but just the same. Normally, however, Blum could deal with this kind of thing. You only had to decide on the right mixture, faster than you'd need to make a salad dressing, of course – a little vinegar but not too much, a dash of oil, but not too little. He produced his identity card and business cards like a conjuror taking a rabbit out of a hat, but anyone looking closely at him could have detected his tension. The conjuror was doing magic tricks to save his life. The policeman did not look closely. He probably still had five more hotels to check.

157

"You're registered in Berlin, Herr Blum. What are you doing in Frankfurt?"

"I'm here on business, Inspector. Here's my card. I'm in the antiques trade. I was taking a look around. Frankfurt still has something to offer in that field . . . but listen, what's all this about?"

"We'll have to check your details. Tomaczek!"

His assistant took Blum's ID card and went off with it.

"You don't mean to say terrorists . . .?"

"I don't mean to say anything. You're staying in this hotel?"

"Yes, of course. I was watching TV." He pointed to the set. The presenter was just closing the programme with the words: "So perhaps this evening may come up with a surprise yet."

The policeman wrinkled his brow. A typical police officer's frown. Perhaps he didn't like the programme either.

"Show me your room."

They went the two floors up. Doors were being opened and shut everywhere; complaints, protests, curses and shouting came from the rooms. Uniformed officers with machine guns were standing by the lifts, staring into space. If Rossi is in the room now, thought Blum, we're all in the shit. In deep shit. His steps became heavier and heavier. Number 523, the Phoenicia. I open the door and we're facing chaos. If it was all connected then the scene would be repeated – shredded mattresses, broken lamps, and what would be sticking out from under the bed? Blum's heart was thudding so loud he could hear it echoing back from the walls. A policeman in a leather jacket stood outside the door. Blum hesitated. The police officers looked at him with bored expressions, but under the boredom their professional reflexes lay in wait.

"I'm afraid it'll be rather untidy," Blum brought out. "I had a visit." He cleared his throat and tried for a grin. "You know how it is. Travelling on business."

The cops looked at him expressionlessly. He was a rat, like all the rest, but a rat with rights – for now, anyway. Blum put the key in the lock, noticed that the door wasn't locked, noticed the police noticing it. They straightened their shoulders. Only a pro would notice that kind of thing. Blum was a pro too: a pro in the art of doing what had to be done. He opened the door.

The window was wide open. The wind made the curtain billow out and slammed the door. To Blum, it sounded like a shot, but policemen were used to shots of a different calibre.

Whoever had been about to search the room had only just begun. The bed was no untidier than after a quickie with the chambermaid, the contents of Blum's travelling bag were scattered on the floor, but that didn't necessarily mean anything either. The man in the leather jacket looked distinctly disappointed. Perhaps he'd expected smashed champagne glasses, shredded silk stockings, the ripe aura left by the inmates of a whole brothel. Or at least an under-age fixer in the bathtub, a girl who would shout obscenities at him while they waited for the duty doctor. The cop in charge went to the open window and looked out. Blum knew what he was seeing – the garage roof three floors below. A pro could make it down. He didn't close the window until he had examined the roof carefully. Then he examined Blum, not quite so carefully, but Blum was only 5 feet 10 inches tall.

"Looks as if someone broke in here. Is anything missing? Take a look."

Blum would have loved to take a look, but to do so he would have had to kneel down in front of the bedside table. He cast a quick glance over his scattered possessions. They didn't look impressive for an antiques dealer. Then he saw that something was in fact missing. His transistor radio. However, he managed to shake his head.

"No, nothing, and I left the window open myself, Inspector. I need fresh air to sleep."

Now the man in the leather jacket was looking around, in the bathroom, in the cupboards, but so casually that Blum realized they didn't really suspect him. To them, he was just a man looking around the flea markets, no better than a shoelaces rep, the mere dust of the big city thrown up and cast aside by the rollers of the sweeping machines in the early morning.

"Are you self-employed, Herr Blum?"

That was clear enough.

"Well, I used to be, but in Berlin, you know, the sheer pressure, the competition, and the economy's not improving."

The scornful looks the officers cast him spoke volumes, a whole encyclopedia full of volumes. No one wanted Berliners now.

"So you're not self-employed?"

"No, I travel on behalf of Träger – Träger in Charlottenburg, scouting around mainly for rugs. Last year I found a Tabriz here in Seckbach, Inspector, in a house clearance sale under a pile of rubble – it was a poem, I can tell you . . ."

His voice was gradually assuming the Berlin accent that the inhabitants of that insular city had cultivated. Blum had been to Berlin when they still had something to cultivate. The police had soon had enough of it, and were glad when his ID card came back. There was nothing to report.

"I could have told you so myself, Inspector."

"Lock your room in future. Frankfurt isn't Charlottenburg."

"I hear you, Inspector," said Blum, laying the Berlin accent on thick.

But when the door was closed it was a full minute before he was in any position to kneel down in front of the bedside table and put out his hand. The key was still there, hair and all, untouched. His heart leaped up. He had to steady his hand to light himself a cigarette, but then he was his old self again. Let them steal radios, he thought. Some never learn their trade.

28

The air was always sultry on level B, even at night, even this night in March. Blum spent half an hour taking soundings. Once you'd been in a *razzia*, you always expect a *razzia*. Under the main police station it did seem to be over, since there was no one around but a few U-Bahn travellers hurrying along the passages, past the boutiques, the pharmacists', the toilets and the dark corners where drunks usually lay in the dirt among their bottles, watching the criminals combing their hair before showing pensioners and nursery school teachers what the underprivileged had on their minds. But today everything was empty down here, and the area with the luggage lockers lay in a ghostly calm. The one human being in sight, a young man in a ski anorak, was studying the pop concert posters outside a cultural sales booth. All was empty even outside the toilets. Blum would have liked to turn back, but he did not intend to spend the night in Frankfurt with 100 grams of coke in his blazer pocket. And he had to feed more money into the luggage locker. He had left the hotel immediately after the police.

"*My plane leaves in three-quarters of an hour.*"

"*Your plane? At this time of night?*"

"*It's a private plane. They're allowed to fly at night.*"

"*Fancy that. May I ask where you're going?*"

"*Vienna.*"

"*Ah, the beautiful blue Danube. How nice. That'll be*

345.80, Herr Blum, VAT included. We must put tonight on the bill, of course."

"And stamp it, would you? You know what the taxman's like."

First he had thrown them off the scent. After a few miles by taxi towards the airport he told the driver he had to look in on his sick aunt who lived in Neu-Isenburg, next exit. The man must surely have thought he was a terrorist, but in ten minutes' time they had reached Neu-Isenburg, and from there he took two more taxis back to the city centre. Expensive, but if you wanted to survive and get anything out of the operation it was no good penny-pinching for the wrong purposes. The man in the ski anorak pushed off. In his place, two drunks came carefully down the stairs. One was carrying the plastic bag with their bottles, the other was smoking a cheroot. A picture of peace. Blum went off to the luggage lockers.

But there were people there now. They had gathered at the back of the place, anyone who had nowhere else to go. A bottle was being passed round, a girl who couldn't be more than twelve was painting her lips, a Turkish lad with a scarred face was playing cards with a mixed-race boy who must be well under age too. About ten of them in all. The level-B kindergarten. They were not happy about Blum. He knew they didn't take their eyes off him. He opened the locker and turned his back to them. He was just stowing the bag of coke in the travelling bag and putting it in with the sample case when a cough made him jump. It was the girl. Her bold, cherry-red mouth was twisted into a malicious grin.

"Got a fag?"

She was beside him, peering into the locker. He put the bag inside and closed the door. Then he held out the packet of HBs. She took two.

163

"Looking for business?"

"What did you say?"

"You heard. I'll do it for twenty. I've got a great ass."

"For heaven's sake, child, get out before I —"

"Before you what? Before you get out your ID. You're a cop, right?"

Finally he had the 1.50 marks ready and fed them into the slot. Then he turned the key and took it out of the lock. The girl followed his movements, hungry-eyed.

"Push off, sparrow."

"Push off yourself, asshole."

Now the boys were surrounding him too. The mixed-race kid put out his hand.

"Give me a mark."

For the church, mister. But this bunch looked a good deal more dangerous.

"Me too."

"Me too."

"And me."

The Turkish boy summed up. "Give us ten marks and it'll be okay."

"Why should I give you ten marks? You must be out of your minds."

"He said he'd fuck me in the ass," said the red-lipped decoy.

"You better give us twenty, then," said the mixed-race boy.

For a moment Blum thought he had lost his reason. Too much coke. He closed his eyes briefly and then opened them. He was still standing in front of the lockers, with the children crowding close.

"Hey, old man, you not well?"

"Looks like he'd fall over any minute."

"I guess he had too much Omo in the stuff."

"Now let me tell you—"

164

"Talks like a cop, but he ain't."

"Hand over the bread, Grandpa, or something nasty might happen."

The drunks were standing silent by a pillar, watching the scene. Blum shook himself. He had dealt with the others. If only this haziness would clear from his brain . . . He tackled the Turk.

"What does your Dad think of you hanging around here, Mustafa?"

The Turk cast him a scornful glance. Then the mixed-race kid joined in, tugging Blum's sleeve.

"Don't try that on, old man. We know what you're doing here."

Blum slapped him down, hard. The others caught the mixed-race kid, and then the Turkish boy had a knife in his hand. Blum hit out, and it fell to the ground with a clatter.

"You've got a hell of a lot to learn before you know anything," he said, but he didn't hang around to teach them. A retreat to familiar territory. You didn't mix it with a horde of precocious teenagers if you had a luggage locker full of coke. The drunks stood where they were, open-mouthed, and forgot their thirst for a moment. Blum waved to them, but they didn't wave back. They had to stick it out even longer on level B. It was cold and rainy up above. Germany was only for those who knew their way around. Blum considered himself one of them, but these young toughs had almost got the better of him. In any place like Calcutta you'd have shown them, he thought, but once they start speaking German you're finished. He went into the nearest snack bar, ordered coffee and a bitters, and took a pinch of coke in the Gents. This was a fine start to the night.

He would have liked to plunge into the commotion of the big city, but Frankfurt was more of a boggy

165

pond; all the flowers grew from the same plant, all the dragonflies danced above the same water. He didn't fancy spending his money on a whorehouse. He needed a place for the night, somewhere to stay during the hours when everything was still in the balance. And since the others knew that too it might be better just to let himself drift. He began drifting.

In the next bar they greeted him as if he belonged there, and a man in dungarees asked if he had another two grams.

"Two grams of what?" asked Blum, frowning, poker-faced.

"What do you think, man? Coke, of course."

"Coke? You mean fuel for your stove?"

"Hey, don't you remember me? I'm Detlev."

"Oh, the anti-nuclear protester. I get it now. Coke instead of nuclear power. Coke power: nuclear coke. Do you build your own nucleus – biologically or with cellophane? I recommend shaving foam. Guaranteed sterile."

Detlev looked at him in horror and retreated. "Wow, man, that's terrible stuff. I'd noticed."

"Really? I was going to change to brown coal anyway."

But of course he couldn't go on clowning all night. Maybe the tragic approach was better. He sat in a bar for an hour, staring at his glass. Then the barmaid asked if anything was getting up his nose, and he left. It was raining. He thought he saw Cora in another bar – same hair, same figure, but she was wearing a long dress – except that when he looked at the woman from in front the effect wasn't so much Bardot as, at the most, Anita Ekberg. Seen too many movies, he thought, and paid. It was still raining. The steel scaffolding on the Opera House gleamed. It was being rebuilt in honour of "Truth, Beauty, Virtue". All very well and good, thought Blum, given a million I'd be with you. Perhaps Cora is right, he thought, and it's no kind of life to be thinking in figures all the time, travelling about in a state of distrust, turning paranoid and insisting on cash. It somehow makes everything dirty . . . right, baby, but what's clean is there to be made dirty, isn't that so? Anyway I'm too old to begin all over again, and if I could I'd probably do the same as before. There's really no point in it, I don't believe in love but I've always paid for it, and when I have my bar on that island some day it will say above the door: All Currencies Accepted. That's a kind of faith too, thought Blum. It had stopped raining. Now it was snowing.

At three in the morning Blum was outside a bar that was just closing, rubbing the snow off his sunglasses with his scarf. A patrol car glided past. The man in the passenger seat looked at Blum. Now he'll report back to the officer leading the manhunt that I'm still out and about, thought Blum. He'll go through my data again, send for the files. Something odd about this customer, he'll think. Look at this, Tomaczek, the man spent a year abroad, we must latch on to that. Telling us he buys up old rugs. One of those fake Berliners, Tomaczek, making out they were there in the fifties. Aha, here we have it! So he was in Tangiers. I can smell narcotics 100 yards away against the wind. Call through to Interpol and connect me up, and you bring in that dealer, Tomaczek, squeeze him till the pips squeak, then bring me what's left and don't forget to wipe the floor clean. With Vim.

A taxi stopped. Two men in long raincoats tumbled out, and they too discovered that the bar had closed. The taxi drove off. They whispered to each other.

Blum realized that one was looking sideways at him. In the wan light they both had pale faces. Snowflakes were melting on their dark, uncombed hair. Blum wanted to move away, but he felt rooted to the spot. Finally the two men came over to him. Junkies, thought Blum. That's all I needed.

"I guess you have something to sell," said the taller man.

"Me? What makes you think that?"

"It's kind of in the blood," said the shorter man nonchalantly.

Yes, they were junkies.

He went back to their apartment with them. Crazy, he thought, but it was all the same to him now. He had the little tube of coke with him. Somehow nothing mattered any more. You had to let things take their course. Take it as it came, go with the flow. It might sound corny but there could be something in it, and drugs had to do with magic. The apartment was large and gloomy, in an old building with a view of the street, trees in front of it. A dirty kitchen, the rest of the place the same as everywhere, the same pointless lumber. Junkies were junkies, that was the only difference. He gave them a pinch, and they mixed the cocaine with heroin and injected it in their veins, right in front of him, brazen as Asian street beggars and with the cold objectivity of surgeons.

"Don't you want to try it too?"

"No thanks, I don't like needles."

"You're missing out on the very best there is."

He shook his head and explored the apartment. The door of one room opened, creaking, and a girl with frizzy red hair stood there blinking in the light of the corridor, clutching an old dressing gown together over her breasts. She struck him as familiar, but he couldn't place her.

"Who are you?" she asked.

"A ghost," he said.

"I've seen you before," she remarked, lighting a cigarette. Her fingernails were very long, and blood-red.

"I feel the same," he said.

"I know where. On the Iron Bridge. You're the guy who had the cocaine."

"And you were driving the tall man."

"Still got any of that stuff?"

They went and sat down with the junkies. The red-haired girl sniffed some coke. Blum asked her why the tall man had called the deal off.

"Oh, him," she said dismissively. "He just talks big. Acts like the Emperor of China, but there's nothing behind it."

Blum nodded. A tram rattled along in the distance. One of the junkies put a record on: reggae.

> "So as sure as the sun will shine
> I'm gonna get my share, what is mine
> And the harder they come
> The harder they fall . . ."

Then they just sat around, and the red-haired girl wanted to go to bed with Blum, but he didn't want any junk or any sex either. All Blum wanted was the money, 200 marks for a gram, junkie money with blood on it, blood money, ashes for snow. The red-haired girl began painting her toenails, and Blum lay down on a sofa and listened to the junkies – one had been constipated for six days, the other was talking about some dirty deal or other, and they both seemed to be discussing the same thing, interchangeable symptoms of the same condition, the same incurable illness. He saw the day slowly dawning behind the trees, the city coming to life, going on again, Frankfurt am Main in the Federal Republic of Germany.

29

The sky in Wiesbaden was bright blue. Blum took a taxi drive through the town twice, to Biebrich and to Dotzheim, until he decided that there was no one tailing him, and yet when he got out at Central Station he had that sense of being watched again. And 100 marks were gone too.

The rollneck pullover he'd bought that morning cost DM 129. A cappuccino cost 3.50. A steak and salad was 17.80. A ticket to Amsterdam cost 104.30. You had to struggle to make ends meet in this country. But that was no reason to double-cross him the way Cora had. He wasn't mixing baby powder with the coke to stretch five pounds to ten. No, you could keep clean even if you were wading through filth, but to understand that you had to be sure of yourself.

There wasn't a word in the newspapers about the big police raid. However, the asylum seekers were making headlines again. Mr Haq had not, of course, been seeking asylum, but a discussion of business and the qualities of modern life. That's no reason to deport someone straight away. My dear Mr Haq, you didn't tell me the whole truth and nothing but the truth, so we're equal but not quits. Tell the barman in the Punjab Club to crush that ice.

The Intercity train to Cologne was announced. Blum stayed on the platform until the last minute, watching the people getting in, but what use was that? Anybody could be one of them.

Blum found a seat next to the corridor. He didn't need to watch the landscape going past. It all looked the same anyway. It was the people who were important. Dangerously important. The well-preserved lady in her seventies with waved white hair who kept her gloves on even when eating chocolate; the bespectacled man with the bush of grey hair accompanying the man with shaky hands who consumed half a bottle of vodka; the thin man in the striped green suit going through a whole pile of model railway magazines with the gloomy expression of someone in his last semester of teacher training – they were the sights worth seeing, the Binger Loch of this journey, the Loreley rock. So he couldn't take his eyes off the corridor for a moment, or put his sample case in the baggage compartment.

The bespectacled man disappeared at Bingen. Before they reached Koblenz he came back without the vodka-drinking man, but with a strong smell of alcohol about him, and as elated as if he'd thumbed his nose at the whole world. The attendant with the drinks trolley came along. Blum bought a coffee. The thin man was hungry, and spent his time over the next thirty miles taking a plastic knife out of a cellophane bag and using it to spread cellophane-packed plastic sausage on a cellophane-wrapped slice of plastic bread. Blum leafed through the Bahamas handbook and informed himself about offshore banking. A pleasing subject, but it wouldn't do to start dreaming about it. The bespectacled man and the thin man would have been a good choice for a syndicate's commando squad. They were definitely filmable. And just because the lady was over seventy didn't mean she was necessarily retired.

Nothing happened in the corridor. The passengers pored over their files, looked out of the window looking bored, allowed the leading articles in the newspapers to lull them to sleep. Blum gradually relaxed. The old lady struck up a conversation about the Bahamas with him. Blum recommended her to invest in Freeport. When he explained the Hawksbill Creek Agreement which had set up the free trade zone of Grand Bahama, the two men suddenly left the compartment. So much for syndicates

"It's too late for me, of course," said the lady at last, "but why don't you risk something on it, young man? Everything here is going to the dogs."

"Madam, it's never too late," replied Blum.

Shortly before they came into Cologne Central Station, the train stopped for several minutes. Blum stood in the corridor staring into a dirty back yard. The soot of a hundred years lay on the walls. A blouse fluttered from a window. Cartons of empty beer bottles stood on the garbage bins. A woman's hand drew a curtain aside, opened the window and brought the blouse in.

Blum saw a man in his undershirt behind her, laughing and raising a beer bottle. Then the window was closed again, and Blum felt a pang in his heart. The train jerked, and came into Cologne Station.

On the platform there were American women with plastic backpacks, Turks with cardboard suitcases tied up with string, sausage-eating commuters, chain-smoking teenagers all wearing the same trousers, the same hairstyles and the same badges, and police informers studying timetables anxiously like travellers fearing that all trains would fail to stop at their station. The Amsterdam train was on time, and Blum found an empty first-class compartment. It was heated, and the red upholstery with its warmed-up aroma of sweat and perfume was reminiscent of the salons of old-fashioned brothels in Algeciras and Ceuta. Blum sat next to the corridor, hand on his sample case.

Two men joined him in the compartment at Deutz, a fat man with a briefcase who sat by the window, and a grey-haired Englishman reading the *Daily Telegraph*. The fat man opened his briefcase and took out a new men's magazine. He moved his lips as he read. If I were still in the porn magazine business he'd be a good customer, thought Blum. Ah, those happy days with the porn magazines, he thought. Söderbaum's "Spring Awakening", those fat Danish tits, all milk and honey – if that was supposed to be perverted, then what was all that out there? He noticed how awkwardly the men sat, either with legs crossed, free hand clasping an ankle, or leaning heavily forward, left hand turned in and propped on the thigh, head bent, and with the right foot curled round the left so as to keep from sitting comfortably, or – like himself – with his right hand clutching his case, a burning cigarette smelling of dung in his left hand, his face red and running with sweat. They were all slaves on vacation, and out there was their district – rolling-mill trains, blast furnaces, atomic piles. Car cemeteries, mines, potash factories. Plastics markets, poison manufacturers, satellite towns, the sun itself a tranquillizer substitute. Housing estate after housing estate, like kraals where the natives danced around a fetish to the shrill howl of the sirens.

The Englishman got out at Oberhausen. The fat man put his men's magazine back in his briefcase, loosened his tie and started studying a sex magazine. The flat landscape was covered with a sulphurous haze. Blum had to go to the toilet. He took the sample case with him. The fat man looked up and grinned.

In the toilet Blum splashed water on his face. It looked to him emaciated and haggard. When he came out into the corridor he saw a man he knew standing

174

outside the toilet in the adjoining second-class compartment. Panic rose in him; his heart raced. He was already hurrying back down the corridor, his case colliding with the doors. The blue suit, the mutton-chop whiskers, the glasses over those froggy eyes, and the fat man with the sex magazine in his own compartment – you see, Blum, we know who you are, you won't escape us. The train was slowing down. A station. Blum clutched his sample case more tightly, and swiftly passed his compartment. He didn't look inside. He would have to abandon his travelling bag, his shirts, his cravat, the Bahamas handbook. The train juddered and came to a halt. He opened the door and looked round. No one else seemed to be getting out. He jumped down on the platform. To his left he saw an EXIT notice and made for it. The station master was already blowing his whistle. The words on a signboard announced: "Welcome to Wesel".

30

Saturday afternoon. Those in gainful employment
were taking their overfed families out for walks. In the
shopping street, they let the mothers and children off
the leash and withdrew with the family dog to a corner
pub. Half an hour to go to the sports show, guessed
Blum. He knew he didn't have much time. His pur-
suers would get out at Emmerich, summon reinforce-
ments at once and start back to Wesel. The others
would stay in Emmerich, at the station, on the roads.
He had to give them the slip again between Wesel and
Emmerich, and for good this time. It would be best if
he got into a train going the other way. Back to
Cologne, and take a plane from there – but where to?
There were security checkpoints and customs barriers
at every airport. No, he must go to Amsterdam. He
could get rid of the stuff at once in Amsterdam. Not
for a great deal of money, obviously, but yesterday
evening he'd have been happy with fifteen grand. And
this way he could easily make 100 grand out of it yet.
The Dutch guilder was a good currency too. The only
problem now was getting to Amsterdam. Taxi? But
anyone going so far by taxi would arouse suspicion. A
hire car was no use. He mustn't leave any documentary
evidence behind him in Wesel. He must never give his
name again.

He reached the cathedral. There was a builders'
fence in front of it, and someone had painted SIEG on
the boards in black paint. A dachshund raised its back

leg and did a pee. A beery twilight prevailed in the marketplace pubs, the jukebox played evergreen hits – "Sonny Boy" – and all who were not cast into gloom on a German Saturday afternoon were assembled on the benches. Blum ordered a Pils and drank it straight down.

"You've got a good thirst on you," said the man beside Blum.

"I guess I've earned that beer," said Blum, looking more closely at his neighbour. The man was a study in brown: dark brown, neatly parted hair, red-brown wrinkled face, raincoat of shimmering green-brown fabric, turf-brown suit, mustard-brown shirt, horse-dung-brown tie. In his brown, fleshy hands the beer in the glass shone like liquid gold. He must be somewhere between fifty-five and sixty, but had no grey in his hair yet, and his eyes were like two blue marbles.

They fell into conversation. Something about the man seemed familiar to Blum, and at the same time he felt intrigued. You could still spend whole evenings discussing beer in Germany, but Blum was in a hurry and quickly moved on to something else. He was a commercial traveller, said the man in brown, a sales rep for a soap powder firm. He trudged round the marketplaces and pedestrian shopping malls of the smaller towns, from the Lower Rhine to the Sauerland, flogging obscure washing powders. Blum could well imagine it: under a damp awning in the pedestrian zone of Neheim-Hüsten, with Spring Awakening soap-flakes and Lambswool detergent, two products which for fifty-seven years had been conducting a hopeless campaign against the giant Henkel company, in front of two housewives with headaches and three school-kids, including two from Asia Minor, on a Thursday afternoon with DM 13.30 in your pocket, and the prospect of sausage with potato salad for supper and a cold bed in the Christian Hostel. If you could imagine it, it didn't mean that the same fate was in store for you, yet a shiver ran down Blum's back, a fear rooted deeper than the fear of any syndicate.

"And who do you travel for?"

"Oh, you mean because of my case – no, I'm not a rep. It's just my things in there."

"In a sample case? Then you must have been a traveller once."

"No, no," Blum assured him. "I've always worked in other lines – the construction industry, restaurants, antiques, magazines, well, anything that came along."

"A lot will come along yet," said the sales rep, "you have a lot ahead of you. I didn't always represent washing powders either."

But he wouldn't say what he had done before. He ordered two more Pilses. Blum looked at the time.

"Not in a hurry, are you?" asked the traveller. "On a Saturday afternoon?"

"I have to go on to Holland."

"What do you want there? The Dutch don't like us."

"But they do business with us."

"Everyone does. That's in the nature of business. And what kind of business do you have in Holland?"

"Oh, I'm – I'm looking around the restaurants. You see, I'd like to open a restaurant myself some time, so I'm gathering information about the kind of opportunities there are in that field."

The sales rep drank his beer and smiled mildly.

"Is that why you're sitting in marketplace pubs?"

"Even if they may not always look it, bars like these can be a goldmine."

"And you'd like a goldmine too?"

"Wouldn't we all?"

"Ah, you still have illusions," said the sales rep, wiping the froth from his mouth. "One does at your age. But when I hear the word mine, I think of the mines that killed our comrades and the trenches where we buried them. Back then in Russia, see? We still had illusions then too. We thought when we came back Germany would be there again."

"And nothing came of that?"

"You know that as well as I do, friend. Nothing came of it. Are you catching the night train, or spending the night here?"

Blum had to pull himself together to find an answer. There was an aura of hopelessness about the sales rep that settled on the brain like murky mist. Yet the man could be useful to him.

"That's just what I'd like to talk to you about. But maybe somewhere else, where we won't be disturbed?"

The sales rep nodded, as if he had assessed Blum correctly from the first. "Let me invite you to supper. Eggs and fried potatoes – I expect you can eat that?"

It was not a question but a demand.

Outside, the mist was grey now and getting darker fast. For a while they followed a country road, and then went a little way along the Rhine. People out walking were standing on the bank, looking west across the river. Crows rose from the fields. A coal barge chugged downstream in the evening mist.

"What happens if you go further on along here?" Blum asked.

"First you reach the lake, the Aue, we're going to turn off there, the campsite won't interest you so much, and then you'd have to go on through Westerheide to Bislich."

"I mean after that. Holland must begin somewhere."

"Are you planning to walk there?"

Blum did not reply.

"Well, yes, then you get to Holland," said the sales rep, with a long sideways look, "but that's quite a way. First you get to Rees, and then Emmerich, of course, and then you have to go over the border. But that's no problem today, the Dutch will let anyone across, so long as he isn't actually stark naked or has no skeletons in his cupboard."

"But you go across often?"

The sales rep shrugged his shoulders and flicked the end of his Reval away. "What would I be doing in Holland?"

"I thought you could buy things cheap there."

"What I need can be bought at home," said the sales rep, thus closing the subject, but Blum suspected that he didn't cross the border for much more pressing reasons.

They left the Rhine, passed a glider club and came into the open country. There was no footpath beside the road, so they went along it in single file, and when car headlights caught them flies danced in front of their faces. Blum began to wonder if he wasn't in the process of losing his reason. Apparently with coke you didn't lose your mind until you lost control over the dosage, but perhaps as a dealer you lost your mind if you lost control over the trade. And you'd surely lost that if you were stumbling along behind a washing powder rep over the plains of the Lower Rhine on foot on a March night, with a mere few marks in your pocket and several syndicates after you. But the air was refreshing, it was a nice evening, there were even stars in the sky. Blum felt curiously cheerful, relaxed, even full of confidence. What were those five pounds of coke in the case, to the handle of which he was clinging as tight as if his life depended on it? They were nothing if he couldn't enjoy every moment as much as this one, totally crazy, almost free.

31

"Enjoy it, friend?"

With his mouth full, Blum nodded. He emptied his plate, and the sales rep cleared away, washed the dishes, and cleaned out the frying pan with scouring powder. A pleasant smell of fat, fried potatoes, bacon and briquettes hung around the sales rep's wooden shed. This, Blum thought to himself, was how the Spartans of today lived – a wooden hut, a camp bed, a roaring stove, a plastic cupboard, egg boxes, plywood furniture, a cheap People's Radio, three rows of paperback classics, the collected works of Karl May. Television sets, refrigerators, best-sellers and women did not feature in the Spartan's life. Instead, he told Blum the tale of the early-nineteenth-century German Wars of Liberation – Major Schill had been executed in Wesel – and did not refrain from drawing bitter comparisons with his own generation's readiness to sacrifice themselves. They had been led astray, lied to, deceived, fooled, seduced, they had given their all – like Schill, like Körner – and those who had the misfortune to survive must bear the shame of fighting in the wrong cause to the end of their days. When had it ever before been wrong and shameful to fight for your own country?

"Don't get all worked up again, Erwin," said the man's colleague, who had turned up after supper, driving a ramshackle delivery truck. His name was Fred, he had small, darting eyes, sparse grey hair and a mouth over-full of teeth. Blum particularly relished the cold beer he had brought with him, and then he discovered they were in related jobs.

"You're right, Fred," said the sales rep. "I know, I know. I ought to keep quiet, quiet till the end, quiet as the Russian graves with the birch trees over them. This isn't my world any more, so why do I bother with it? Since Germany ceased to exist I don't have a world any more."

"Erwin was once at the top of the tree," said Fred, close to Blum's ear. "The very top of the tree." And he winked, as much as to say: you know what that means, because now we're at the very bottom.

"But Germany is still beautiful," said Blum. "I've just been on a little business trip – it seems a pretty flourishing place to me. And we have no less than two Germanies."

"That doesn't count," said the sales rep briefly. "Neither of them counts. The golden calf and Bolshevism, that can't be Germany."

"Perhaps a mixture of them?"

"A mixture! Mixtures, that's the washing-powder culture, my friend. No, there's no point in it, but of course one should never give up. What did you say you were transporting?"

The brown man's glance was still friendly, but he now looked quite hard in the light of the naked bulb that hung from the ceiling. His contours were sharply outlined. He chain-smoked Reval cigarettes and stubbed them out in a metal container of a shape that reminded Blum more and more of a steel helmet.

"That's what I wanted to discuss with you," said Blum. "I'm looking for a way into Holland where there won't be any checkpoint. Not on account of the police, I can always manage them. But the Federal Criminal

Agency, you understand, those lads are clever, they don't do things by halves. There could be problems if they take a close look at me at the border. And that wouldn't be a good idea at all, see what I mean?"

He laughed, helped himself to another can of Dortmund Actienbräu, and pulled the tab off the top. The head was like the foam in the jumbo cans. He toasted the two colleagues. The sales rep nodded gloomily; Fred's quick eyes swivelled towards the sample case.

"Federal Criminal Agency?" asked Fred. "Isn't that . . ."

"State security," said the sales rep, relishing the term.

Fred looked at Blum, frowning. Had he gone rather too far? Blum raised his hands.

"I want to be on the safe side," he said. "I really can't afford to make mistakes."

His eyes moved over the sample case. The sales rep coughed his way through a couple of Revals without taking his eyes off Blum. His friend Fred drank his beer, looking nervous.

"Slow and easy," he said. "I don't want anything to do with state security. You have to admit, Erwin, we're out of our league there."

The sales rep narrowed his eyes and stared through the smoke, perhaps seeing graves with birch trees whispering above them, or perhaps just the damp tarpaulin next Thursday in Neheim-Hüsten, and the housewives staggering out of the supermarket with their ten-pound drums of Ariel.

"The man has to get across the border," he announced, "and so he shall. No one must be lost. That's what we're here for after all, the last of us."

They looked at one another, Blum and the man in brown. They did not entirely understand each other,

184

but at least they knew who they were. And Blum saw himself in twenty years' time, worn out, in a place like this, without any Wars of Liberation, with a fridge and TV in the evening, before shoelaces were abolished world-wide.

"Don't you have any schnapps, Erwin?" asked Fred. "I feel kind of cold."

As he spoke he looked sideways at Blum, as if he were responsible for the chill in the air. But the sales rep had no schnapps. He put another briquette in the stove, for the benefit of Blum, not Fred. Small-time crooks, his manner suggested, wouldn't quote state security at you.

"It'll soon be the same old story, load your ammunition, they won't get me alive. And all for a sack of potatoes, eh? That's what I call inflation."

"I can pay," said Blum.

The sales rep made a dismissive gesture, but Fred was thinking along more practical lines.

"Good ways across are few and far between," he pointed out. "We can ask a kind of fee, right? You have to look at the practical side, Erwin."

They reminded Blum of an old married couple – the idealistic champion of mankind's better instincts whose wife has been nagging him for the last forty-five years about the neighbours, neighbours long ago fixed up with official positions and sinecures, and now their block was occupied by good-for-nothing heathens. Finally he settled the matter with a 100-mark note, and Fred remembered that he still had a bottle of spirits in his glove compartment. While he went to fetch it the sales rep cleared the beer cans away, and as he slipped his coat on he said, "I hope you get through safe and sound, friend. Yes, the battle's still worth fighting at your age, never mind what for."

"You're not on the scrapheap yet, not by a long way," said Blum.

"I'm sixty-two, and after thirty-five years of this I'm just about ready for the scrapheap. Here, take the torch, I expect you can use it, but go easy with it. The batteries are running out."

"I don't know how to thank you," murmured Blum, putting the torch in his jacket pocket.

"Do me a favour and don't let Fred crack up," said the sales rep, looking at Blum with his blue eyes. "He's the only person I have left."

"I won't," said Blum. Then Fred came back with the spirits, and they all had a drink, and Fred had another, and then they left the sales rep's hut.

The sky had clouded over, and a cold wind had risen. The delivery van bore faded lettering: F. KOWALSKI – BEST EGGS, FRESH CHICKENS – BISLICH, LOWER RHINE. They squeezed themselves into the driver's seat, Fred behind the wheel, the sales rep next to him, Blum by the door with his case between his knees. During the drive a loose piece of metal somewhere kept clanging, Fred had difficulty changing gear, and the heating wasn't working. So they juddered on, sticking close to the Rhine, under the sulphurous sky that never allowed complete darkness to fall, making for Holland. No one said anything. Blum was sorry he hadn't taken a pinch of coke. He felt unutterably weary and dispirited. At this crucial moment, he thought, of all times. He could deal with these two colleagues, but if the Italian was waiting for him again in the first Dutch town he reached he'd probably have to give up. He took a deep breath and lit a cigarette. No, he was not about to give up. Federal Germany had almost done for him, its damaged, hopelessly corrupt citizens like Cora. That was all behind him now. See it through, he thought.

See it through. Even if he landed up in Neheim-Hüsten in the end, he might still see Freeport first, maybe even the Punjab Club in Lahore, with Mr Haq . . .

"Wake up, friend," said the sales rep beside him. "We're there."

"At the border?"

"We have to go a little way on foot now."

Blum clambered out of the truck. Fred was standing behind a hedge relieving himself. The truck was parked at the far end of a little wood with a gravel path running past it. The sky was already pale on the horizon, and birds were beginning to stir. The sales rep stood close to Blum.

"Watch out for Fred," he whispered. "He's got his eye on your case."

Blum nodded. He looked at the time. Nearly four. The bastard's been driving us around for three hours, he thought. Fred waved. They walked along beside the wood, first Fred, then Blum, then the sales rep. After quarter of an hour they came to a stream. Fred and the sales rep, who were wearing gumboots, simply waded through the water. Blum took a run and jumped. He made it across the stream without losing his case. They went on, zigzagging through a little wood, across fields and meadows, and finally reached a footpath leading straight into the mist.

"Go along there and you'll come to another stream," said Fred. "Then you're in Holland. Follow the stream and it leads to a canal on the left, then you come to the road and you can catch a bus."

It was beginning to get light. Blum looked hard at Fred, the case in his left hand, his right on the handle of the knife in his jacket pocket.

"And suppose someone spots me? There must be border guards patrolling around here."

He saw Fred smile. The sales rep was now standing on his colleague's left.

"Nonsense," said Fred. "And if they are – I thought they couldn't touch you?" His gaze wandered to the case, his left hand to his coat pocket. "I'd love to know what you've got in there, friend."

"You're welcome," said Blum, ramming the case into Fred's stomach, while the sales rep seized his left arm and held it tight. Fred groaned and swore, but not very loud.

"Good thing you noticed he's left-handed," whispered the sales rep.

"I didn't," whispered Blum back. He did not shake hands with the sales rep but waved to him after he had gone twenty yards. The sales rep was still hanging on to Fred's arm.

"Do you want to know what's in it?" called Blum softly.

"What?"

"Dynamite," called Blum. Then he walked quickly away down the path without looking round again.

32

Blum lay on the bed, staring through the window at the roof of the building next door. Two seagulls were perched on the chimney. It looked as if they were staring back. He heard the hurdy-gurdy from over at the Damrak Hotel playing the same tune all day. The sky was a dirty grey.

He picked up the phone, waited for reception to answer, and said he'd like to try the Frankfurt number again. He read it out once more from the card that Hackensack had given him, although he knew it by heart. The card was dirty too now. And once again he heard the ringing tone and imagined the phone in an empty room – cleared, abandoned everyone gone, only the yellow crocus still shining on the wall. Suddenly there was a crackle on the line. At first Blum thought the connection had been broken, but then a voice actually spoke, a male voice.

"Hello?"

"Hello, Mr Hackensack. Blum here. You remember me – Blum –"

He stopped. Hackensack would have reacted by this time.

"Is that you, Mr Hackensack?"

"No, this isn't Hackensack." But the speaker was American too, that was obvious. "Who are you?"

"I'm a – a business partner of Mr Hackensack's. I was at your office last week. I spoke to a lady there."

"Where was this?"

Blum named the street, the number of the building, the floor, the name of the firm, and described the mummified Prussian secretary.

"Ah, well, that lady isn't with us any more," said the man at the other end of the line. "We never heard about your visit. What was it you wanted to discuss with Mr Hackensack?"

"He was going to advise me on an investment. Meantime I've already made one, but there are certain problems with further developments, if you follow me."

A pause, then: "Maybe."

"Can I speak to Mr Hackensack personally, please?"

"I'm afraid that won't be possible just now. Mr Hackensack isn't here. We're having some difficulties with our reorganization."

"I see. But perhaps you can give him a message?"

There was a rushing sound on the line, and Blum thought the man had hung up, but then he heard him again. Quite close this time.

"That can be done. What did you want to say to him?"

"Tell him I'm in Amsterdam and I'd like to get in touch with him. Tell him it's about chemicals . . ."

"Chemicals?"

"Yes, he'll know what I mean. Chemicals and information. I'm at the Hotel Roder Leeuw."

"And what was your name again?"

Blum spelled his name.

"I hope you don't mind waiting a little longer, Mr Blum."

"Listen . . ."

But the man really had hung up now.

Blum took a packet of cigarettes off the wash-stand. Fishy smells wafted out of the kitchen of the hotel restaurant into the inner courtyard, and fat pigeons were waddling along the gutter. The bells of the Nieuwe Kerk were playing the "Ode to Joy" again. Beethoven on the half-hour, some Protestant hymn or other every hour, Blum suspected. There were multilingual warnings about hotel fires in the Roder Leeuw too. *Do not panic. Keep calm.* Easier said than done, thought Blum. It was raining now, and the raindrops too were natives of a country where the cooking was good; they were fat and smeared the window. He lay down with his cigarette.

The room was smaller than anywhere he had stayed since Barcelona, furnished only with the bare necessities, the mustard-coloured fitted carpeting in the man-made fabric supplied to all hotels of this category, and a coloured print on the wall showing a canal in Amsterdam at a time when you could still bathe or catch fish there without dying of poisoning. The water dripped from the shower-head in the shower cubicle. The wardrobe door wouldn't close properly, and although he had turned up the heating he was freezing, even in his rollneck pullover. After an endless, nerve-racking day he had reached Amsterdam utterly exhausted, taken a room in the first hotel he found and slept for a full day, and when he had woken up it was another day before he could bring himself to go out and eat. He felt like a limp sack of flesh with its muscles on strike and its brain sending out no more signals. Perhaps the nocturnal sessions with the voice broadcasting those coded instructions into the ether had taken over his unconscious mind, and now, here in Holland without a radio, cut off from the secret frequencies, he was like a missing agent slowly dying in the cold.

They're keeping me on ice, he thought as he stared up at the dirty sky by day, and when he woke from dreams of terror by night, drenched in sweat, and heard the "Ode to Joy" again as he gulped down a glass of water; trembling, he thought: now they're going to grill me. And when he heard the telephone ringing and ringing in Frankfurt, he saw Hackensack, fat Mr Hackensack, Consultant, sitting in a similarly shabby hotel room in a similarly dilapidated town, trying to tune radios that were no longer broadcasting, speaking into phones on a dead line. Then Blum said, out loud, "You just need the right attitude, Mr Hackensack," and he laughed and stubbed out his half-smoked cigarette and turned to the wall, lapsing into the new but ever-familiar nightmare that always began on white beaches and always ended in flight, in ruined cities under dark moons, among frogs with killer eyes and blondes with blood-red lips.

And all the time the sample case of cocaine stood unlocked under the wash-stand, and once, when Blum had just opened it and was looking at the jumbo cans, the Indonesian chambermaid came in with clean towels, and he took a can, showed it to her, sprayed a quantity of foam on his cheek, and the chambermaid laughed, she had beautiful eyes, and for a moment even that was possible again, but then she put the towels down on the wash-stand, he picked up his shaver, she went out of the room, and the hurdy-gurdy played its tune for the seventy-seventh time that day.

33

Blum went out for a Chinese meal. He found a decent-looking restaurant, quite empty, in a street on the outskirts of the Old Town. An old man with four long white hairs wafting over his polished bald pate like strands of candyfloss brought him sharkfin soup, mushrooms, fried shrimp and rice wine. Alone in this large restaurant, under all these lamps, among Buddhas and gilded dragons, attentively observed by a company of silent, smiling waiters, Blum felt for a wonderful moment like a traveller who is the first to set foot in an undiscovered country, and is treated by the natives with that exquisite courtesy which leaves the stranger unsure whether he will be accepted as a friend or chopped up at night and fed to the pigs. This moment, unfortunately, did not last very long, for another customer entered the restaurant.

The young man – Blum judged him to be in his late twenties – was greeted by the Chinese respectfully but with obvious familiarity, and sat down a few tables away, his face towards Blum. He did not so much as look at the menu, but listened to what the old Chinese waiter was whispering to him and then nodded. He wore an old tweed jacket and jeans, his fair hair fell untidily to his narrow shoulders, and there was reddish stubble on his thin face with its watchful eyes. But even the way he lit his cigarette spoke volumes to Blum – the young man had exactly the provocatively casual manner that he himself had done his best to cultivate all his life.

Blum turned his attention to his meal again. All the same, he could see that the young man had only a bowl of soup and then ordered coffee. As he pushed his plate away and was wondering whether to have a coffee too, he saw the young man take out a small snuffbox, sprinkle some of its contents on the back of his hand and sniff it up with enjoyment. Then he grinned at Blum as if to say: well, friend, what do you think that was – Pöschl's Brazil or Peruvian flake? Blum immediately took his little tube out of his trouser pocket and imitated him: left – right. And then again, left – right. The Chinese waiters acted as if they had seen nothing.

"Good stuff?" asked the young man, stirring sugar into his coffee. He spoke with a Hamburg accent.

"We could swap – you let me sniff yours and I'll let you sniff mine."

The man from Hamburg stood up and took his coffee cup over to Blum's table. His face looked a little older at close quarters. A few wrinkles already, and rings under his eyes.

"So the old man actually brought you something to eat," he said, sitting down and crossing his long legs.

"Why not? This is a restaurant, isn't it? Our slant-eyed friends make a living by serving food."

"Haven't you noticed how crowded this place is?"

Blum lit an HB. If this man wanted to tell him something then he needn't bother with an answer. It was superfluous anyway, and the Peruvian flake was just taking effect and rocking his head. The man from Hamburg was staring at the wall where a picture hung.

"Sensible of him to hang a picture of the Boxer Rising over it, don't you think?"

"Over what?"

"Over the blood that sprayed on the wall."

"Blood? What blood?"

"Blood and some brains too. Three weeks ago the Israeli Mafia drove up here one evening and stopped the whole Chinese heroin trade at a blow. But not quite the way the Narcotics Department imagined. Still, it looks perfectly civilized again here, don't you think?"

"Very civilized. And the cooking is excellent."

"Yes, Mr Lee served the best Cantonese food in Amsterdam."

"Served? Was he at the table too?"

"The police fished him out of the Amstel next day with his big toe in his mouth. But the restaurant was shut for only three days. And the day it opened again three Israelis were found in the garbage bins of the Hilton with their throats cut. All with their pricks in their mouths. Amsterdam is an interesting spot for anthropologists. Too bad for the Chinese that one of the Israelis was a member of Shin Bet, their secret service. Since then it's been very quiet in this restaurant."

The fair man snapped his fingers, and one of the younger waiters brought him another coffee. Blum finished his rice wine, but it wasn't strong enough for him any more.

"You know your way around," he said. "Been here long?"

"Oh, for ever. Of course Amsterdam is always interesting for certain trades as well as for anthropologists."

"So long as you can get along with the Israelis."

"And the Chinese. And the Moluccans. And the Turks. And the anarchists."

"Anarchists? What do they have to do with it?"

"Oh, the anarchists have made up the leeway pretty well. They could flatten half the city, but they'd rather rake in the subsidies first. In a few years' time, if all goes well here, you won't be able to move except in a helicopter, preferably a Vietnam-tested American Huey with a troop of rangers firing at anything that moves – first a canister of teargas over the rooftops, then gas-masks on and into the office with an escort and a barrage of firing . . . a little scuffle before every deal will raise the most sluggish blood pressure . . . no, seriously, when it gets hot here you can forget everything you ever heard about street fighting. Once the lid comes off the pan you'll be able to smell it all the way to the Bahamas. Another little pinch?"

Blum shook his head. He had a feeling that the lid was coming off his own pan. "You don't by any chance know a blonde called Cora?"

The young man smiled, pleased. "Oh yes. And you must be Blum, right?"

"How did you know I'd be here?"

"Pure chance."

"Oh, really."

"My name's Ted." He beckoned to the old Chinese standing by a screen with a toothpick in his mouth and staring at the Boxer Rising.

"And I always thought there were no coincidences in this line of business."

Ted paid the bill. "I assume you'll come back with me for a drink. We'd almost given up hope of finding you."

"We?"

"My partner and I."

As they left the restaurant, the Chinese stood in a row like a reception line, and the lights were switched off. No sooner were they outside than the iron shutters came down. On the corner Blum noticed a car with two radio aerials outside a cigar shop. Two men were sitting in its dark interior watching the Chinese restaurant, and Blum caught himself feeling something almost like relief. Other people had their problems too.

Ted drove an old Volvo. They did not talk much on the way. They left the car beside a small canal and jumped aboard a houseboat. The water smelled of decay. A yellow cone of light fell out of the cabin.

Ted knocked on the door, giving a signal, and it was opened from inside. The first person Blum saw was Cora, sitting on a floor cushion and looking expectantly up at him.

"Hello, baby," said Blum, and he went in.

34

Blum would have furnished a houseboat in just the same way – top quality Oriental rugs, comfortable seating in the corners, a stereo system, a bar. All that struck him as strange were the three cuckoo clocks hanging on the wall above a number of Far Eastern knick-knacks. They were part of the business, explained Ted's partner, a youngish, dark-haired character called Tim.

"Our warehouse is elsewhere, of course – since yesterday, in fact, we have two warehouses. Decentralization sometimes makes sense – but the cuckoo clocks do a fantastic job in discussion with customers. I mean, some people practically faint away with delight hearing those cuckoos every quarter of an hour, three times running, timed to exactly a ten-second interval between each other. The Japanese flip their lids."

"You sell cuckoo clocks to Japanese?"

"I told you these two were something special," said Cora. Blum looked darkly at her.

"We just brought the cuckoo clocks back with us," said Ted. "They're made in Kuala Lumpur. We often do business there. Malaysia is practically our hinterland."

The pair of them seemed to deal in anything eccentric – cuckoo clocks, walrus harpoons, opium pipes, electroplated staples from Taiwan, military tags from Singapore, translations of the Koran into Burmese, remaindered stocks of lace underwear from bankrupt Italian fashion houses, dry batteries from Uzbekistan. They also obviously smoked an Afghan hookah pipe and drank Bloody Marys by the pint. And then the little doors in the cuckoo clocks opened up and the cuckoos started calling. At ten-second intervals. Cora lounged decoratively between a burning candle and a sleeping cat, pretending to be drawing. Even more silver had flaked off her cowboy boots, but she was now wearing an expensive and exotic silk blouse, no doubt from Ted's stock. She seemed to be on very intimate terms with the two dealers. A dealer groupie. Blum was ignoring her, which made her nervous. The conversation was now revolving around cocaine – Peruvian flake, 96 per cent.

"Good stuff," said Ted, who had taken a pinch and was cleaning his nose. "But at present the market's chaotic. That makes things a little difficult."

"How much of it do you have?" asked Tim.

"Didn't Cora tell you?"

"Cora just said it would be a shame if you didn't turn up."

"I still have about 2,400 grams. If you take it all, of course I'll give you a special price."

"How much do you want for it?"

Blum named a sum in guilders. He noticed Cora looking at him. The two dealers exchanged glances. Here they went again – singing the same old song.

"And I have to insist on cash, boys. With a discount like that you'll see it has to be cash. If possible in large notes, but of course I'll take smaller denominations."

The two of them smoked their cigarettes. The cuckoos performed their aria, but Blum was not a Japanese.

"Can't you turn those things off for a bit?"

They were turned off. Cora was drawing as if oblivious of her surroundings, but she didn't fool Blum. The cat had woken up and was washing its paws. It was an ordinary black domestic cat, but it had a white spot on each paw, to which it devoted at least as much attention as a belly-dancer to her beauty marks.

"So if you can't do business in cash," Blum summed up, "you can forget the deal."

"I'm thinking of the guano," said Ted slowly, looking at Tim.

"Good idea. Killing two birds with one stone."

Blum cleared his throat. Cora's pencil hesitated. "Guano?"

"That's right," said Tim. "At present prices I'd put it at about 125,000 guilders."

"The only drawback is, it's cruising around somewhere in the South China Sea," said Ted, "but we won't let that stand in our way."

"It's a question of logistics."

"Exactly. Do you have that last telex somewhere?"

"In my head. Coming into Macao, dated 17 March, Captain Willems or whatever his name is. Absolutely reliable, Blum, you needn't have any unnecessary suspicions. If Willems sends a message to say he'll be in Macao on such-and-such a date, you can set your watch by him."

"If you happen to be in Macao. Another Bloody Mary?"

Blum put his hand over his glass. This was not the moment for strong liquor. His veins seemed to be swelling, and his voice sounded unnaturally loud. "What's the idea? You want to give me guano in exchange for the cocaine?"

"Do you know what a pound of guano is worth?"

"St Laurent would pay any price for it."

"That shit they use to make perfume?"

"You only have to fly there and take over the cargo. From Willems or whatever he's called."

"In Macao."

"I don't believe I'm hearing this. You two must be trying to pull my leg."

The cat stopped licking itself. It looked attentively at Blum. Cora too had stopped pretending she had nothing but art in her head.

"No need to get so worked up," said Ted. "The guano is ours as soon as it reaches Macao. A simple forward transaction, understand?"

"Since when does one have to go and take receipt of the wares personally in a forward transaction?"

"They're not pulling your leg," said Cora. "You can trust them, Blum."

"Like I could trust you, right?"

She looked him straight in the face and pouted. Slut, thought Blum, but he suddenly felt a pang at his heart. He drew on his cigarette. The pang passed over. They always passed over, except the latest. Ted cleared his throat, and the cat returned its attention to its paws.

"Let's stick to business," suggested Tim.

"We must integrate you and your stuff in our current deals," Ted explained. "All deals are parts of a complex system, like interlocking cogwheels. The cocaine has to be a part of the machine, like the guano or that cargo of new Japanese torches our agent in Hong Kong has rustled up for us – switch them on and you see a naked woman, and there's Jane Birkin moaning, '*Je t'aime.*' "

"That's nothing new," said Blum. "I popularized them myself when I was at school. Anyway, I haven't the faintest wish to be a little wheel in your big machine—"

"With five pounds of cocaine you wouldn't be exactly a little wheel—"

"— or a big wheel either. I don't want to be a wheel at all, understand? I never did want to and I never will."

"But you are. Everyone's a wheel. And all of us together —"

"Listen, boy. Not me. I'm my own business. I always have been. Always a one-man firm. No one under me, no one above me, no one beside me. Just me. I've always managed perfectly well that way. And I'm not planning to change my system in the future. Get it? No commission, no forward transaction, no cheques. I get paid in cash. Always. On principle. Direct methods. The direct way."

"Oh wow," said Ted, "spare me that individual capitalism stuff, it belongs in the early eighteenth century."

Glances were exchanged. Then Cora said, "And I thought you'd get on so well with these two. You and your figures and agents and Bahamas —"

Blum rose, emptied his glass and put it down on a stack of old issues of *Fortune*.

"You weren't listening to me, Cora. You were too busy going behind my back. Supplying Hermes with information. Just tell him I still have the stuff. And I'm operating on my own. Blum still has it and Blum will sell it yet. To the highest bidder. Cash and carry. The old method. Well, you know where to find me."

"You'd be a real hit in Macao, Blum," said Ted, and Tim started the cuckoo clocks again. The cat had turned its back on everyone and gone to sleep. It too was a one-man firm. Blum closed the door behind him. It was the only thing to do. And now back to the cocaine, the cold category D hotel rooms, and nights in combat against the cartels. You were the only person you could be, and you did it, you stayed that way. It might not always be a good feeling, but it was all you had, so you accepted it.

35

The bar was in the middle of the Old Town. It wasn't exactly the Pegasus Bar in the Phoenicia, and it certainly was not the bar Blum was planning to open once he had found his island, but the beer was cold, and odd characters didn't bother him so long as they kept themselves to themselves. He was drinking his beer, staring at a circus poster on the wall and thinking of nothing in particular, when a man wearing a hat pushed his way in between him and the odd characters at the counter. Glancing at him sideways, Blum immediately knew what he was, and why. This man too was flotsam washed up in these surroundings, with his shabby raincoat, Trevira suit, striped tie and some fifty-five years of the struggle for survival showing in his face: the bags under his eyes, the wart on his cheek, the wrinkled turkey neck. But his eyes were still in search of something, and his chin wasn't done for yet. Another traveller, thought Blum, on the long journey from Solingen to Neheim-Hüsten by way of Stalingrad, but this one still believes in the Bahamas, just as I do. Or perhaps Ascona is more like it. The man nodded to Blum, raised his hat – Blum noticed his heavy black signet ring – and ordered a gin in Dutch. When he turned to Blum he spoke German. He had a husky smoker's voice.

"Nice bar," he said, tipping back his gin.

"Nothing much wrong with it," Blum agreed.

"You from Germany too?"

"You can hear I am."

The man nodded, and ordered another gin. "One for you as well?"

"I'll stick with the beer, thanks."

"Very sensible."

"Yes, beer is the only reliable thing."

"Beer and cash in hand, eh?"

"You're dead right."

They drank for a while, and then the man said: "Nice city, Amsterdam."

"That depends," opined Blum.

"Do you visit it often?"

"When business brings me."

"May I ask what your line is?"

"I'm an agent," said Blum.

An interested glance, another gin. This old soak certainly wasn't bothered about his liver any more.

"That's a wide field," said the man at last. "What do you deal in, as an agent?"

"I take what comes. Mainly chemicals and information. And what's your line?"

"I'm in the import–export business."

"Ah. Do you know Frankfurt?"

"Who doesn't?"

He should come out with it now. The key words had all been spoken. Perhaps there was still one missing.

"Then you'll know the ICA, I expect?"

"ICA? Which fair is that?"

Got it wrong, then. Ah well, you can't always win. But it was about time for something definite in all this obfuscation.

"Forget it. Comes under the heading of information."

A tart with blue hair started towards the man, but he dismissed her with a glance.

"Information is too vague for me, see? I prefer dealing with concrete things."

"Like tropical fruits? Spare parts? Plastic bags?"

"More or less. It depends what's in the plastic bags."

The eyes were the same as those that had sent the tart packing, but now they were the eyes of an innocent angel. Careful, Blum.

"Most plastic bags have chemical items in them."

"You can say that again."

"Not that chemical items have a very good press, these days."

"Ah, well, in my line the products of the press are simply for wrapping up the goods. And you don't survive long in our kind of business if you're prejudiced, am I right?"

"Just what I always say myself. Have another gin?"

"Thanks, yes. But I suggest we move somewhere more comfortable, okay?"

He's right, of course, thought Blum. I can hardly broach the subject of five pounds of coke in this dump. Even the arses have ears here, and not every weirdo confines himself to singing Verdi arias or "Stranger in the Night". On the other hand, if the man isn't working for Hackensack he could be just sounding things out. Blum drained his beer glass. He looked around again, but saw nothing that represented an alternative. Perhaps this was what the advertising people called the drugs scene – the blue-haired tart now devoting her attention to two American sailors, the Chinese hermaphrodite with a pigtail, sucking the end of it, a thousand years of torture in those lashless eyes, the leather-clad yobs talking big about the number of cops they'd chew up next time round, the ethereal disco girls, stars in a sky where no natural sun now shone, the people gawping in the corners – but it was not

Blum's scene. He had never been a part of it, and strange as it might seem, he was less a part of it than ever now with his five pounds of cocaine. At that moment he would have given something to know where he did belong, but as no one could tell him he paid for his beer and followed the man with the hat and the wart and the import–export business out into the street.

36

"What kind of a man is he?" asked Cora. She was sitting astride the only chair that the Hotel Roder Leeuw allowed the guests in its single rooms, watching Blum pack. Not that there was much left to pack, but Blum had a considerable talent for making an elaborate ceremonial even out of stowing away two pairs of socks and a toothbrush.

"A small businessman," he said thoughtfully. "A loner like me. Grey hat, grey suit, grey voice. Import–export business."

"A character like him isn't going to buy five pounds of coke straight off, just like that. These things don't happen. For cash, too."

"Cash down, yes. Look, to you the word cocaine doesn't mean the same as it does to his sort. You see it as exotic, of course – magical, mystical, gift of the gods, Paradise White, the White Lady, all that stuff. I'm not saying it's entirely beside the point, but for normal businessmen cocaine is just a commodity like any other. What does illegal mean today? At least it's more profitable than shoelaces or staples. Good business."

"Normal businessmen don't deal in coke, Blum."

"What does normal mean? Since these aren't normal times you can hardly expect ordinary businessmen to be the only normal people around. Selling staples, dried petfood, inner tubes. Think of your friends Ted and Tom."

"Tim. Ted and Tim."

"Yes, well, I . . ."

"But they're eccentrics, they're putting on an act."

"Not everyone in a grey suit is a sober citizen, Cora, and I personally can only laugh when you say your friends are doing it just for fun."

"I didn't say that. But you don't know them. You didn't want to get to know them either. You simply ran for it when everything wasn't going exactly as you wanted – cash down on the table, a done deal, off you go."

"Either Sekt or seltzer water, that's what I always say."

"Then you've been drinking an awful lot of seltzer water recently, you poor thing. Have you finished packing yet?"

"Take it easy, little one. What do you want to do, then? Fuck?"

"Sometimes you make me want to throw up, Blum. But somehow I like you all the same, and I didn't betray you. To anyone. I don't know why you ran away from James like that, but you never stick around long enough for anyone to explain anything. Except when you're packing, then you take your time. And now this so-called businessman – I see how it is, he waved a few banknotes at you and now it's yes and amen to everything. And later you'll feel insulted because he's a cop after all. Haven't you thought of that one?"

"You really think I'm naïve, child, don't you."

"And don't keep calling me child."

"What else do I say? You don't like baby either."

"You're crazy – baby, child! Haven't you noticed that I'm a grown woman?"

"Not losing your sense of humour, are you?"

That was payback for the seltzer remark. He took off his ankleboots and held them up to the light. It was nearly mid-day, and a strip of spring sunlight shone on one side of the roof outside. Cora had been here for an hour, and he still didn't know why. He dampened a towel with hot water and rubbed his ankleboots till they shone. Cora smoked and stared at him.

"All right, neither of us is naïve and we haven't lost our sense of humour either. That man's not a cop, Cora. A businessman, say he's gone broke ten times, he simply says to himself, I'll never get my villa in Ascona by legal means so let's try the narcotics, maybe that's better than the used-car business or a dry-cleaning outfit. There are plenty of his sort around. They don't all start dealing in drugs, but after a while they get to thinking of it. It's not the exclusive affair it was ten or twenty years ago, with a lot of fuss and bother. The fuss and bother is just for the poor bastards who do themselves in with the stuff."

"Sometimes you talk like a cop yourself. Are your boots clean yet?"

"If either of us is like a cop it's you, Cora. It takes a cop mentality to let yourself be planted on me, to spy on me. And who for? For a narcotics pro like Hermes. Or was he only putting on an act for the hell of it too? And who says you haven't been planted on Hermes by the cops. Where's your police tag, Cora? Third jacket pocket from the left?"

Her face froze. Two tears dyed with mascara ran down her cheeks, drawing two fine lines on her skin. She stared at him, her hands clutching the chair back, her white knuckles standing out. Blum turned away and put his boots on. When he looked up again she was reaching out her hands.

"Help me, Blum!"

He stayed where he was.

"Help me, you idiot! My legs have gone to sleep, I can't stand up! Blum!"

He pulled her up, the chair fell over, and of course she landed in his arms. Gone to sleep nothing – she was pressing close to him, trembling, hot, her ash-blonde hair crackling, then they were lying on the bed, he below, she on top of him, her eyes closed, like a parachutist leaping from a plane. But Blum was not a cloud, nor was he going to be the meadow on which the bold conqueror of the heights might land.

"I have to leave, Cora. Really, this isn't the moment."

"You wanted us to stay together once."

"That was before I knew what your job was."

"Aren't you making it a little easy for yourself?"

"Is that what it looks like? Do I look as if I'd ever made things easy for myself? The deal will finally go through in an hour's time – I'm only risking a couple of years or a knock on the head – and here I am lying with you on this bed which is creaking under us, and you're working on me with your lies, claiming I make it easy for myself just because I don't fall for your line."

"Hermes had a hold over me. I owed him something. And I told him you didn't have any snow. I —"

"Because you wanted it yourself. You and your nice clean fashion photographer, you wanted the whole five pounds for yourselves, that's why you didn't tell Hermes anything."

"Oh, for heaven's sake, if I'd wanted your coke I'd have it by now! Do you really think I didn't know where the key to the locker was all the time? Do you think I'd have needed someone like James to get at your stuff? You poor fool, you thought we were all after your pathetic bit of Peruvian snow the whole time."

"Well, you are, admit it. You must see it's no use soft-soaping me."

"Is that what you really think? Weren't things ever different between us?"

"I don't believe in that any more, Cora. I don't believe in us."

"I need you, Blum."

"You're crazy. You don't need any clapped-out desperado with receding hair and a sample case full of stolen coke."

"And how about you? You think you can do it alone. You know you can't. Let's at least try. Working together we have a chance."

"No, not together. We have even less chance together than working alone. Anyway, I don't like sharing – either the profits or the expenses."

"Is that your last word?"

"We're not on stage, Cora."

"Do you have to make everything sound ridiculous?"

"I don't think your role in all this was particularly amusing, but I expect I'll be having a good laugh about it in the end."

"I didn't give you away, Blum."

"Perhaps not. But that was your role."

"I told you, Hermes —"

"Cora, I don't want to hear your side of the story any more. When I did, you said you didn't have any stories, there weren't any. And now I don't have any desire to hear them. Or any time either."

"No, you never have time. You do make things easy for yourself, Blum. You let yourself off lightly when it gets serious. You let your friend Mr Haq down too. Speedy Blum rushing from date to date. Do you remember how I told you in Frankfurt you ought to just leave the coke in that locker? The stuff does for some people because they take too much of it. And it does for others even when they're only selling it."

"And you say I make things easy for myself. Look, Cora, I really do have to leave now."

She made no effort to get up, so Blum rose on his own. She just looked at him.

"Blum like a flower in bloom, no first name. But you're missing more than a first name."

"I'm not missing anything. Only money, same as most people. Come on, Cora."

Even the most persistent have to give up some time. She painted her pouting mouth pink and slipped her fake fur on. Then she took a piece of paper out of her shoulder bag, put it on the wash-stand, looked at him once more with a strand of her ash-blonde hair falling between her big grey eyes, and disappeared. He stared at the door. Funny girl, Cora. First you saw girls like her as a dream, then you realized they were performing plays of their own. But life seldom doled out the best parts. He looked at the piece of paper. It was a drawing, a delicate line drawing in coloured pencils. He was mixing drinks in his bar down by the harbour, wearing a Hawaiian shirt. Even the awning was there, the words Bahamas Bar stood over the entrance, a parrot was perched on the counter between the peanut machine and the little barrel of rum, exactly as he had imagined it, and Cora was in the picture too, just coming down the steps into the saloon, waving to him as the drinkers at the bar raised their heads, and Blum – the Blum looking at the drawing – recognized in them all the people from whom he had fled.

37

Blum paid and got out of the taxi. A school class was just leaving the zoo. Their teacher was urging them to hurry, because the rain was beginning again. It had kept raining from time to time all through the middle of the day. A cold breeze blew from the harbour, and an old man with a beret and a dark coat was standing at the ticket office in front of Blum. The cashier seemed to know him; they were having a little chat. A regular customer. Patience, Blum told himself, and lit another HB. I mustn't attract attention now. In the end he was allowed to shell out his own couple of guilders. The man with the beret disappeared into the reptile house. Blum went on, past the enclosures for the big cats. It was raining harder. The sample case of coke gleamed wet. Blum looked at the time. On the dot, in spite of Cora. He kept his left hand in his jacket pocket.

Outside the elephant enclosure, a Javanese with a lot of gold jewellery was taking a photo of his Dutch girlfriend, a blonde with a receding chin. Probably a bombshell in bed, thought Blum. His steps were slower and slower. By now it was impossible to over-look the symbolism: the narcotics deal in the zoo, and in front of the cages of captive animals the trap was closing on him too. Although the customer had wanted to meet him in the Rijksmuseum, and the zoo had been Blum's idea. There was the man now, over by the aviaries. The hell with it, thought Blum, he's as nervous as I am. His hat was on the back of his head, his tie loose, his dark glasses looked ridiculous. But he was carrying a similar sample case. Two young girls were looking at the eagles, an Indian in a turban was talking to an Indian without a turban, otherwise there was no one to be seen except for a keeper pushing a wheelbarrow full of garbage away.

"There you are," said the customer, clearing his throat so much that Blum could hardly understand him.

"I almost didn't recognize you with those glasses on," said Blum.

"Oh, the glasses. You think they're too conspicuous?"

"You must know they are."

"Then I'll take them off. And the case . . .?"

"Yes, it's in there. And do you have the money?"

"Ha, ha, that's a good one! Did you think I'd come with a load of poker chips?"

"Show me, then."

"Shall we go a little further . . .?"

They went a little further and found a bench, but the Indians were strolling along behind them. They stopped in front of the bench. The Indians stopped too, gesticulating vigorously.

"Could look a little odd sitting on a bench in the rain. This wouldn't have happened to us in the Rijksmuseum."

"There are far too many people there," said Blum.

"But we're going to get drenched!"

"Do you have a better idea?"

"Let's go into the monkey house. It's dry there."

"But it'll be crowded there too."

"Just a few schoolkids, they won't bother us."

"You like monkeys?"

"I heard the gorillas here are really enormous."

So that's where the trap's to be, thought Blum. In the monkey house.

Not only a shady character, tasteless too. If a man was a criminal at fifty, did he have to be a tasteless criminal at fifty-five?

He nodded. "I like gorillas myself."

They made for the monkey house. Blum glanced back. The Indians were just settling down on the bench. *Chacun à son goût*. A couple in leather jackets and blue jeans were disappearing into the monkey house. Blum stopped.

"What bad luck. Those two know me. From the hotel. It wouldn't be particularly clever to do it in there."

The customer looked bothered. "So what do you suggest?"

"Let's go over to the big cats' house."

"No, I can't stand the stink there."

"Look, don't you feel this is getting ridiculous? We're doing a 50,000-mark deal, and you get worked up about the stink of the big cats . . ."

"I never liked the idea of the zoo anyway."

"Let's go into the reptile house."

"Why not the café?"

"Oh, come on, for heaven's sake! In a café! How many witnesses do you want?"

"We wouldn't have had any witnesses at all in my hotel room."

"No, just three gorillas to knock me out."

"Your suspicious nature isn't making things any easier."

"We'll go to the reptile house. Or do have you anything against crocodiles too? Did you know crocodiles have existed for 18 million years? They've seen so much already that they won't take any interest in our dirty little deal."

The customer looked decidedly alarmed. He was clutching his sample case in one hand and using the other to hold on the dark glasses that kept slipping off his nose.

"You're planning something. The reptile house. Why the reptile house? Do you have your friends waiting there? Is that where you're planning to snatch my money?"

"Who's talking about a suspicious nature now? You have persecution mania, you do. How am I to know you have the money in your case at all?"

"And how am I to know you have the – the stuff in yours?"

"Well, let's go to the reptile house and take a look. You can see how hard it's raining. We're looking really ridiculous! You get my case, I get yours, and if everything's okay you never need step inside the zoo again in all your life."

"Who ever heard of doing a deal in the zoo!"

"There's a first time for everything. Now, let's go. We've been standing outside this bloody monkey house far too long."

The customer, a bad case of nerves, was sweating. "Then I'll take a look round the reptile house first," he said. "I have to feel it's safe, you understand."

Poor bastard, thought Blum, he's cracking up. Well, I can understand that. Let him. Either he has the money, in which case you can afford to wait a minute yourself, or he doesn't, and then it makes no difference anyway.

"Okay, I'll give you five minutes and then follow you in."

The customer nodded, straightened his glasses, and went back the way they had come, walking much too fast, going past the enclosures with the beasts of prey to the reptile house. Blum followed him slowly, an HB in his hand, drawing greedily on it from time to time. The Javanese was now taking snapshots of his fiancée in front of the flamingos. In the rain and the dim haze, he looked the one truly exotic creature in this twilit place full of jungle flora and fauna, but Blum had only to glance at his sample case to know that there could be nothing more exotic than a man of around forty in a wet blazer, walking into the reptile house of Amsterdam Zoo with five pounds of cocaine inside cans of shaving foam, hoping to strike lucky at last. Unless it was his customer, the man of fifty-five with his Trevira suit and his dark glasses, searching the reptile house for hidden hitmen.

A puma from the Andes lay in its cramped cage in the corner, but when Blum stopped in front of the bars it rose and looked around, as if searching for some way of escape. Was it coincidence? There was no coincidence involved in this game. He looked at his watch. Perhaps only two minutes had passed, but never mind – he couldn't wait any longer.

A class of schoolchildren was pouring out of the reptile house, and it took Blum some time to get through the entrance into the low-built, long building. The reptiles were behind glass on one side of it, and on the other side behind bars and lying in basins of water, in a sultry, putrid miasma meant to simulate the atmosphere of alligator swamps and the banks of the Nile. Blum's customer was nowhere in sight. The reptile house was empty except for the man in the beret who had spent so long chatting at the ticket window. A crocodile fan. He was standing by the basin containing the really big ones. Blum went over to it too. The stench was overwhelming. Perhaps the old man was absorbing the swampy climate as a rejuvenation cure, because he didn't look quite so old now. Blum addressed him in English.

"Did you see a man wearing a hat? He must have been in here just now."

The man cast Blum a brief glance, but said nothing.

"A friend of mine, you see. We were going to meet here."

The man glanced fleetingly at Blum's case, and then said, also in English: "Yes, there was a man in here, but he obviously didn't like the air of the place." He smiled. "A lot of people don't." The smile disappeared. "He suddenly went berserk. Very regrettable. There were children in here. They took him away."

"I think you're lying to me," said Blum.

The man shrugged his shoulders. "What do I care about your friends? I come here to look at the animals."

He turned his back on Blum and walked slowly on. Blum stared after him, and then examined the basin of crocodiles. Some were drifting in the muddy water, others lying by the verge, crawling over each other, opening their jaws, eyeing each other without moving, waiting – but it was a timeless waiting, a waiting that had lasted 18 million years. Blum turned and left the reptile house.

The rain had suddenly stopped. The sky had actually cleared. The Javanese was standing at the kiosk by the exit buying a stuffed toy tiger as a souvenir for his fiancée. Blum made his way through the turnstile. A man came towards him. That feeling of panic again. The lookout man . . .

"Mr Blum? I was asked to give you this."

He put an envelope into Blum's hand, and next moment he had disappeared. Blum couldn't have said what he looked like. He opened the envelope.

Will expect you at 20.00 hours tomorrow
Roxy Bar, Ostend
Best wishes, Harry W. Hackensack

38

When the train crossed into Belgium Blum heaved a sigh of relief. He had had quite enough of Holland for the time being. Even the cows looked more normal in Belgium. The little country railway stations with their rusty ads for Stella Artois and their sooty brick buffets, the railwaymen's housing estates along the canals, where children were fishing and geese walking through the lush grass, the smoke from factories ripe for demolition that merged with the soft grey light to form a misty veil – it might not be Miami, Maracaibo, Macao, but it was what Blum most needed after all this insanity. Sober peace and quiet.

His only companion in the compartment seemed to feel the same way, for it was not until they were over the border that he took off his blue plastic raincoat and put down the book he had been doggedly reading ever since Amsterdam. Then he took a pure white handkerchief from the inside jacket pocket of his black suit, carefully cleaned his rimless glasses, and spoke to Blum in unctuous tones. Blum shrugged his shoulders.

"Sorry, I don't speak Flemish."

"Ah, you are German! I am delighted, of course."

"Why of course?"

"The Germans have done so much to spread the word of the Lord. Do you have toothache, sir?"

"Yes, all of a sudden. Like someone exploring the root with an icepick."

"Well, I am no medicine man, and I can't give you dental treatment, but I can pray for you."

"I wouldn't like to impose on you."

"Oh, but why? Prayer, you see, is a force-field linking us to the divine grace. Prayer awakens us to healing, so Duncan Campbell taught."

"What was his name again?"

"Our teacher Duncan Campbell, the great Scottish preacher, Herr . . .?"

"Schmidt," said Blum.

The man had a head much too large for his small, thin body, encased in black cloth beneath which he wore a black pullover leaving the collar of a white shirt free. There was not an ounce of fat on his face either, but great energy lay around the narrow mouth and the hard blue eyes. He offered a bony hand.

"And I am Brother Norman."

His handshake was like a steel clamp. These lunatics were a perfect pest. And this one a cleric into the bargain!

"Where did you learn German?"

"Oh, I've had plenty of opportunity. And we have a large community in Germany."

"I see. What's your church, if I may ask?

"The Church of Prayer, Herr Schmidt. As Duncan Campbell taught us, prayer is the unifying force-field in which all the barriers that have separated human beings for so long are removed. Let me see if I have a German edition of our little introductory pamphlet in my case."

"Oh, please, don't trouble. I travel light, you see."

"I'm sure a leaflet will fit into your case, Herr Schmidt."

Wasn't that a rather insinuating look? Never mind, the train was passing through the suburbs of Antwerp, and Blum had to change here.

"As it happens, my toothache's gone away. So you did help me. Pleased to have made your acquaintance, Brother Norbert."

"Norman. Are you getting out here?"

"Yes, I want to have a look round Antwerp."

"And where are you going then, Herr Schmidt?"

"Well, I'm on holiday. Just travelling about at random. Goodbye!"

Blum got out of the train and strode off to the station buffet, where he ordered sandwiches and coffee. At about this time two weeks ago he had been going down to St Paul's Bay with the Australian. *Verbum dei caro factum est.* Odd, religion followed you everywhere, it kept on intervening. He took the picture of the Virgin Mary out of his breast pocket. It was rather damp and had a slightly mouldy smell. *Madonna salvani.* Still, it had lasted this long, which was more than you could say of many human beings. He put the little picture away again and patted the sample case affectionately. We'll soon find the right place for you, baby. Blum will look after you. We'll soon be there. He hadn't felt so cheerful in a long time.

As he was making for the Ostend express, he saw Brother Norman waiting on the next platform. Find someone else to preach to. He went to the front of the train and made himself comfortable in a first-class carriage.

On the way through Flanders the sky grew darker and darker. In Ostend a strong wind was blowing, there were showers of rain, and gleams of sunlight over the sea. Blum handed in the case at the left-luggage office. Now he had a left-luggage receipt again. He put it in his wallet with the Madonna. A Sealink ferry was just leaving the dock. The sea air refreshed Blum. He walked past the docks to the

222

Visserskaai, which led to the promenade. The Old Town lay beyond.

The bars smelled of fish and chips. Tourists stood outside the souvenir shops, holding on to their umbrellas and converting Belgian francs into English pounds and German marks. Blum determined not to let himself be palmed off with Belgian francs. You'd never get rid of them except in the casino. A poster announced a performance by Shirley Bassey, another a lecture on the Bermuda Triangle. Blum felt almost at home. Suddenly there was a heavy shower. Large black mastiffs were racing along the empty beach. Ebb tide. Time for a drink. And there was the Roxy Bar. A reddish neon sign promised REAL ENTERTAINMENT. It was only five-thirty, but Blum was always susceptible to such temptations.

39

The Roxy Bar proved to be a shabby hostess night-club. Dim lights illuminated a long, narrow room like a tunnel. There was a kind of bar at the entrance, and niches on both sides of the long room containing plastic-topped tables, wooden benches with worn cushions, small lamps with plastic shades. On the walls, which were papered in a clerical strawberry red, hung dusty pin-up photos, while the long tunnel of the room ended at a small platform with an old piano on it, and Blum wasn't sure if the two women in aprons and headscarves scrubbing the platform represented Real Entertainment or were cleaning ladies. Intoxicated sales reps and seamen sat in some of the niches, complaining of their fate or of the girls here, who were dozing or telling jokes in loud voices. A jukebox was belting out a hit, and the smell was like the atmosphere of a second-class waiting room.

Blum turned to a grey-haired man in a stained waiter's jacket standing behind the bar, adding up receipts. A long white scar adorned his simple face. A woman somewhere in her mid-fifties looked at him with suspicion. She was in full warpaint, with a large bead necklace around her neck and a Titian-red wig on her head. Her fat fingers with their brightly coloured rings, their nails filed to sharp points, were playing with a cola glass still one-third full of a liquid that looked like a mixture of eggnog and Pernod.

"Excuse me," said Blum, "I heard this was the best show in Ostend."

The barkeeper looked up from his receipts. He had just shaved, but had cut his upper lip and forgotten to remove the scab of encrusted blood. He looked at Blum and seemed to like what he saw, for he bared what remained of his brownish teeth, but before he could say anything the woman in the Titian wig placed her hand on his arm, and turned to Blum, speaking in a surprisingly soft and melodious voice. You could tell she was a trained singer.

"You flatter us, mister. But if a man can flatter as nicely as you do nothing good usually comes of it. May I ask who told you so?"

"A friend."

"I see. A friend. Perhaps we know your friend?"

Blum gave a description of Hackensack. "And he always wears striking hats, and he drinks bourbon like water."

"No, doesn't mean anything to me. Most Americans wear peculiar clothes, you know, and they all drink spirits like water."

"Perhaps you'll get to meet him. We arranged to meet here this evening. Can you reserve us a table?"

She let go of the barkeeper and nudged him in the ribs. He beamed.

"Get the gentleman a drink, Joseph! What would you like? Are you an American too?"

"Do I wear peculiar clothes?"

"Well, they're a little lightweight for this climate."

"Oh, I don't mind that. I'm German. I'd like a beer, please."

"A beer, Joseph. German beer!"

"We ran out yesterday."

"I'm happy with Belgian beer."

"Fine. But if you reserve a table you must reserve two girls as well. Tables only come with girls."

"Of course. And is there a show this evening too?"

"We have two shows every evening, at nine and eleven."

"Then I'll reserve a table for both shows."

He put a banknote on the bar. She took it, giving Blum a rather odd look. "Not going to make any trouble, are you?"

"Madam, I don't know the meaning of the word trouble."

"I just had a kind of feeling when I saw you come in."

Joseph had opened the bottle of beer, and the madam poured half a glass for Blum.

"But I don't mind that," she said, clinking glasses with Blum. "Trouble can be amusing too. Your health, sir!"

"And yours, ma'am."

They drank, and then she said, "Why not take a table right away? We could be so busy later we run a bit short of girls. Or you'll have nothing but business in mind, such things have been known. Come along, amuse yourself first, who knows what will happen later? My husband – God knows he gave me grief, but at least I have to admit he never failed to show women they came before business. Well, what about it? Would you like a table?"

Blum glanced sideways at the gloomy niches, the swathes of smoke with nowhere to disperse, the puddles of beer, the plaintive drunks. Compared to this, the Playgirl on Malta where the cockroaches screwed in the jukebox was a fun, swinging place. On the other hand he didn't fancy walking around the town, rain was beating against the door, and at least it was warm in here.

"I'll send a good girl over to you," said the madam, pouring more beer into his glass, "something very special. Amuse yourself a bit – who knows when you'll next get the chance?"

"Very well," said Blum, "a little atmosphere can't hurt. But let me know when the American arrives."

He winked at her. She smiled back. No sooner had he sat down at one of the tables than a Eurasian girl appeared with another beer for him and some lemonade for herself. Looks as if the madam really does mean well, thought Blum. Mona, as the Eurasian girl was called, was half Chinese, half French, and her face, although bloated with alcohol, still showed traces of animal beauty. Her olive-coloured skin gleamed like grease. Her thick lips, which could have been a black girl's, left Cora's pouting mouth in the shade. She had cut her black hair very short, so that it lay on her flat skull like a bathing cap. Her plump figure was clad in a green trouser suit embroidered with red glass beads. Blum even liked the barbaric costume jewellery on her short fingers. She sat enthroned on the wooden bench, a Chinese tourist demon sipping something called a sherry cocktail and cleaning her nails with a toothpick, while Blum began to sweat. She was the Great Whore, the Angel of the Harbour. *Madonna berikni u salvani.* From Valletta to Ostend in fourteen days, from Helga the dentist's wife to the imported Mona, from a case full of porn magazines to a case full of coke. But it wasn't the cases that mattered, perhaps they were even a nuisance, perhaps a man about to be forty tomorrow should travel without any baggage at all in future. There was something bleak and ghostly about the Roxy Bar, and something in the Eurasian girl's eyes that sent a shiver down Blum's spine – a great void, an emptiness. He asked where she came from.

"Saigon," she said, giving him a provocative look. "But my father, he great general in China, he go back to

Shanghai to save fatherland, they take him prisoner, he still in prison. When I have much money I free him."

"Perhaps I can help you," said Blum.

"You? Why you?"

"Well, perhaps I'd be glad if someone got me out of prison too."

"Why you in prison?"

He grinned, wiped the sweat from his face, drank his beer. "We're all on a knife-edge."

"Yes?"

"I mean, we can all tread in the shit any moment. Bang, and they lock you up for ten years. I don't think I'd mind if there was someone wanting to get me out."

"But my father general, he in prison for China."

"Surely it doesn't make any difference after thirty years."

To Mona, however, it did make a difference. By comparison with her father the general, anyone else who had to go to prison cut a poor figure. Blum tried to imagine Hermes being shown in a good light by his daughter – if she really was his daughter – telling her customers about him in twenty years' time in Hamburg or Marseilles. She couldn't very well say he was in prison for Germany. Anyway, men like Hermes very seldom ended up in jail. They had not just their numbered accounts, they had their escape routes too.

"What you think of, Bloomin?"

"Blum. Like a flower in bloom."

"Bloomin."

"This'll make you laugh, I'm thinking of money."

"Why? You can't pay?"

"Of course I can pay, Mona."

"For sherry cocktail?"

"Would you like another?"

"No. For me can you pay?"

Of course he could pay for Mona too, said Blum, but wouldn't that spoil their friendship? No, he could pay her all the same, said Mona. After all, she didn't need the money for herself, she could live on bread and water, she could live on air if she had to, no, she needed it for her father the general who had been all alone in prison for thirty years, forgotten by everyone but his daughter because the prison was so secret, nobody knew where it was, somewhere at the other end of the world, but once he had smuggled a letter out, a letter that had reached her a year later. And he had written that all was not lost, he had built a sundial in the prison yard, and he had taught birds to speak, and the rats brought him food. Could Blum do that? Yes, said Blum, if he had a daughter like Mona he could do it too, and he'd have found out that all was not lost in Istanbul at the latest. And Mona smiled, or at least two small lines appeared one on each side of her mouth, but it was still a smile. If you had nothing else, that was happiness.

"Now we go to private room," she said.

The "private room" was a surprise. In the part of the Roxy Bar where clients made love it was a good olf-fashioned bordello with well-heated rooms and pink wallpaper, lavishly supplied with pot plants and velvet-covered doors, Turkish ottomans and French beds, candelabras and gilt-framed trick mirrors. Perhaps Blum had underestimated Hackensack's taste, but the dust lying everywhere showed that the fashions of the nineteenth century had few followers today in Ostend, as elsewhere.

If no expense had been spared on the furnishings, Mona spared none either. She kept enticing new desires and new banknotes out of Blum, and she herself even had moments of pleasure and made strange sounds, like the twittering of birds, so that Blum wondered what kind of man that father of hers must be, and what birds he had taught to speak. Finally, bathed in sweat, he laid his head between her thighs, on her wet pussy, and in his thoughts he was far away in China when a cold draught of air from somewhere swept through the room. He opened his eyes. A man in a white suit stood in the doorway. Somehow the man seemed familiar. Then a second man made his way into the room through a door in the wallpaper. He wore a leather jacket and seemed less familiar. At the same moment Mona pushed him away from her and disappeared through the door in the wallpaper. Blum sat up and rubbed his eyes. He had almost forgotten about this character.

"I take it you've finished," said Rossi, closing the door behind him.

40

"You're making a mistake, Rossi," said Blum.

"Is that all you have to say to me?"

"I don't have the cocaine."

"Why are you lying, Blum? We've been watching you ever since Amsterdam. The case is in a left-luggage locker, and the locker receipt is in your wallet."

They'd been watching him since Amsterdam. Not since Malta, then, not since Munich, not since Frankfurt.

"And how did you know I was in Amsterdam?"

"Amsterdam is a small city, Blum. A thing like that gets around."

"But the frog-eyed character in Frankfurt wasn't your man?"

"I don't know what you're talking about."

"Can I get dressed?"

"Please do."

The Italian leaned on the wall beside the door and watched as Blum dressed. His partner, looking bored, was leafing through a comic book. Blum's movements were rather slow. It took him a whole minute to put on a sock.

"I don't have all evening, Blum."

"One really ought to put on clean underwear after screwing."

Rossi didn't answer but inspected his fingernails.

"I have the case, yes, Rossi, but the stuff isn't in it any more. Who'd go to Ostend with cocaine? No, I gave it to some people in Amsterdam. It was making me too nervous."

"If you're looking for your other sock, it's hanging from the vase of flowers."

"Oh, so it is. Smart dollybird, that Mona. How did you know I'd be going to the Roxy?"

"Anyone who knows you slightly can count off the likely places on the fingers of one hand. Ostend's nothing but a village."

"Then all that was intentional – with Mona?"

"You can wonder about that until your life's end. Which won't be too far in the future, given the mistakes you're making."

"What kind of mistakes? I mean, okay, admittedly it may have been a mistake to take the left-luggage receipt from your – er – wig . . . and I see you have the wig back again . . . but anyone would have done that."

"Your biggest mistake was not selling the cocaine at once."

"No one had the money. And I can't complain. I had a good time."

"At my expense, yes."

Rossi helped himself to the whisky that Blum had had sent up. Blum sat on the bed and tried to get his boots on.

"So what's going to happen now?"

"Guess."

"Why didn't you get the stuff off me in Amsterdam?"

"We wanted to see what you'd do with it. But you're so nervous, Blum. Here, have some whisky."

Meanwhile Blum was putting his jacket on. He felt the weight of the knife.

"And in case you have any kind of clever trick in mind," said Rossi, as if he had guessed Blum's thoughts, "forget it. Francesco here is a karate black belt."

Francesco made a jerky bow and then returned his attention to the comic book. Blum was dressed now. The white suit looked good on Rossi, although Blum himself wouldn't have worn a chequered tie with it. Italians weren't what they used to be. He still hadn't given up all hope of the coke yet.

"Right, Blumo," said Rossi, "let's go and get that stuff now. Give me the locker receipt."

"Think again, Rossi. I handed the case in only three hours ago. The man will remember me. It'll be best for me to do it myself."

"Okay. You may even be right. But don't forget – you have no chance of getting away with the stuff now."

"And what's going to happen when *you* have the stuff?"

Rossi's smile matched his brutal chin.

"I'm sure we'll think of something. *Andiamo*, Blum."

It was just after eight now. They left the Roxy through the door in the wallpaper, down a corridor and out of a side exit. It was raining again. Rossi the great coke dealer had an American car, but he didn't fool Blum that way. This is out of his league too, he thought. The neon lights of the bars and restaurants were flickering in Lange Straat, then the dock lay ahead of them and the outline of a ferry was in their headlights.

They turned into the railway station forecourt. The car stopped. They got out. Rossi went ahead, Francesco kept close beside Blum. Two American women were just handing in their backpacks at the left-luggage office. Blum took the receipt out of his wallet. One Italian to his left, another to his right. As soon as he had the case in his hands he must do something, but he had no idea what. He could hardly kick up a racket. But if he did nothing the five pounds of coke would be gone for good. The American women got their left-luggage tickets but still stood about near the office, studying a map of the town. Rossi nudged Blum.

"The receipt, Blumo."

Blum gave the man on duty the receipt. He saw three other men standing about at the back of the left-luggage office, smoking and looking at the three strangers. There couldn't be a lot to do in the Ostend left-luggage office on a Friday evening. While the left-luggage man was still looking for the sample case, Blum had an idea. He turned his head and whispered to Rossi behind him: "Rossi, police!"

He felt Francesco twitch. Rossi nudged him again, gently.

"Don't talk nonsense, Blum!"

The man put the sample case on the counter.

"I don't have any Belgian money, Rossi."

Rossi put the money down, the official gave him change, which Francesco pocketed, and Blum reached for the case. This was the moment, but he could think of nothing to do. The Americans were in the way. They walked around them, and then, at the same time, they saw the man standing in the doorway of the buffet just treading out his cigarette.

It was Larry the Australian.

"He's a cop, you idiot!"

Blum was already in motion, still with the case, and then everything happened all at once: Rossi's partner tried to attack Blum, Larry tripped him up, a man in a raincoat stood in Blum's way and snatched the case from him, the American women screamed, a uniformed policeman caught Rossi at the exit, Blum stumbled and was caught by Larry, Larry whispered something in his ear that he couldn't make out, they were already crowding out of the concourse, the Italians flanked by policemen, Blum by Larry and the man in the raincoat. Larry had the case now, the ferry sounded a signal, rain was running down Blum's face, and he had just one thought in his head: this is finally it. Curtains for you in Ostend.

He was steered into a car, Larry sat in front, two men beside Blum in the back, hard, expressionless faces, no handcuffs, but what would be the point? They had him.

The cops won out in the end. You imagined a bugbear and it came to life. And here was Larry as police chief, a narcotics agent, of course. Making out he'd been in Vietnam. You could believe it of him. They drove off. Blum felt himself falling down a black hole. Everything was giving way, there was nothing to hold on to, he was tumbling, plunging. Jail. He wanted to scream, but he couldn't utter a sound. How much did you get for this? Three years? Eight? Ten? He wouldn't survive even one year, not at forty. It would be all over tomorrow.

The car stopped somewhere, in a dark quarter of town, huge cubes of empty hotel blocks, he could hear the sea, it was high tide. They entered one of the cubic buildings, neon lighting, a lobby, looked like a hotel, carpets, chandeliers, the lounge, of course, these were no ordinary cops. Larry could be grinning, the bastard. I'll take you to Gozo with me, you'll be safe from your girlfriend there. The dentist's wife. Oh Madonna, no more women. How long for? No woman for three years? For eight years? Ever?

I'd rather be sliced up small. I'd rather die.

Lift, corridor, carpets muffling their footsteps, the bearded man in the windcheater going ahead with the case, the sample case, the case with the coke inside it. He opened a door, waved Blum in. The raincoats stopped. Why did you have to do everything they wanted, even go through this door? They pushed you, so you went in, and there sat Hackensack in his shirt and suspenders, sipping a glass of whisky.

41

Except that it wasn't whisky Hackensack was drinking but apple juice, and on the table behind which he sat enthroned a long row of pillboxes, packets of tablets and ampoules of liquid had been set up. A bright green plastic cap was perched on his head, giving his face a wan, unhealthy colour. Even his nose looked pale.

"Well, that went quite smoothly, Mr Blum. What are you staring at me like that for?"

Blum had to swallow again. He couldn't utter a word.

"Ah, you're surprised to see this pharmacy. Yes, my doctor has put me on a regime of apple juice and chemicals." He began taking his medicines.

"One for the liver . . . one for blood pressure . . . one for diabetes . . . one for the circulation . . . one for my stomach . . . one for my gut . . . once you start mixing with quacks you never break free of them . . . one for my metabolism . . . and you, Mr Blum, have made a considerable contribution to my state of health . . . need anything yourself?"

"No, thank you," Blum managed to say. "If I remember correctly we were going to meet at the Roxy Bar."

"Yes. That way we got rid of the man Rossi."

Hackensack drank some more apple juice from the bottle, put it down as far from him as his arm would reach with a look of the utmost dislike, donned a pair of reading glasses and leafed through a file.

"And now for you, Mr Blum. Blum, Siegfried, born 29 March 1940 in Butzback, Upper Hesse." A faint smile flickered across his face, which seemed to have lost a few rolls of fat since Malta.

"Isn't the penitentiary somewhere near there? Well, never mind. From 1961 to 1963 you studied art history and economics in Berlin. Why did you break off your studies so abruptly?"

"Do I have to answer that?"

"No, you don't. But I'm trying to build up a picture of you."

"They were lasting too long."

"There, you see? Then you went to Wiesbaden and opened a gallery there. Blum and Bloskowitch. But that lasted only three years. Was that too slow for you too?"

"We went bust."

"What kind of art did you deal in?"

"Old art, Mr Hackensack. What is all this? An interrogation?"

"Oh, come, Mr Blum. Interrogations are conducted only by the police and other state authorities. I'm a businessman. Wasn't this art mainly fake icons?"

"Icons are icons."

"In 1969 we find you giving a brief guest perform-ance in Istanbul. What were you doing in the meantime?"

"Taking an active part in the political movement."

"You mean those porn magazines you produced in Copenhagen in 1968? But why are you standing all this time, Mr Blum? Larry, give him a comfortable chair. You two know each other, after all. And you should remember Brother Norman too . . ."

Sure enough, there by the door sat Brother Norman in his black suit, with an encouraging smile on his face. There were three of them – Hackensack, Brother

Norman, Larry. The sample case stood on the table beside Hackensack. Blum sat down and lit a cigarette. This didn't look like ten years in the cooler. Or was it going to turn out to be something much worse?

"The money we hoped to make from the porn magazines was all to go into the political movement, Mr Hackensack."

"Please, don't make yourself ridiculous, Blum. You pulled a fast one on your partner, that man Söderbaum, and you went underground with the porn magazines. Only recently you were hawking the last of them around the whole Mediterranean area like beer past its sell-by date."

"Tastes have changed."

"Yes, indeed. Then came Istanbul, then the butter affair, then the antiques scam, faking antiques was the only thing you'd learned . . ."

"Faking them? Oh, please! I don't know the first thing about faking antiques. I simply bought the stuff in."

"And recently you've been rather going downhill, a little job here, another there, you've even waited tables, and in Tangiers and Tunis you sank so low as to let yourself be kept by women tourists."

"I'm not going to reply to such scurrilous accusations, Mr Hackensack."

"You don't need to. Your story speaks for itself, Blum. A story with a predictable ending. Anyway, then you met up with this Rossi on Malta."

"Through your henchmen here."

"I always say the power of coincidence is the greatest power on earth."

Here Brother Norman opened his mouth. "I can't remind you often enough, Harry, there is no such thing as coincidence. In God's force-field we are the iron filings brought together by the magnet of Providence."

"Right on," said Larry.

"I really could do with a bourbon at this point," sighed Hackensack. The Australian produced a silver hipflask from his windcheater and handed it to Hackensack, who took a long pull and licked his tender lips with relish. Then he offered the flask to Blum.

"Is this the second phase of the interrogation?"

"Oh, cut it out! All this stupid talk of interrogations, Blum! It just shows you have no idea what you're talking about."

"How am I supposed to take the present conversation, then?"

"I told you, I'm a company adviser. Naturally I don't just advise companies active in commerce and industry. I still have plenty of contacts from the old days, after all, so now and then I advise outfits of a more political nature."

"I don't quite see you as an adviser to terrorists, Mr Hackensack."

"Who said anything about terrorists? I'm talking about governments, Blum. Take the case we're concerned with right now. I was recently able to do the Belgian government a big favour by helping to close a leak in their investigation into the narcotics trade. My price? Well, we'll see how the evening develops. But don't forget, when you go out through this door, the Belgians impose severe penalties on drug smuggling too."

"What are you getting at? I don't have the stuff any more. You have it."

"Yes, and it was one hell of a grind getting hold of it. All the agitation I've had these last few days isn't good for my heart. I'm not getting any younger."

"Prayer is the best medicine, Harry," Brother Norman remarked. Hackensack looked at Blum.

"Brother Norman means well. I don't know what I'd have done without him in Vietnam."

"He was invaluable in Casablanca too," said Larry, and went into a coughing fit that lasted at least three minutes. Maybe I've been in my cell for quite a while already, thought Blum, a cell in a building with the words Municipal Madhouse over the door. Hackensack's sausage fingers were fidgeting alarmingly. Blum saw a ring that looked to him familiar on one of them. Of course – it was the black signet ring worn by the customer he had lost in the reptile house.

"You have a new ring, Mr Hackensack."

"Yes, a customer gave it to me."

"My customer, wasn't he?"

"And what a customer too, Mr Blum. The man has eight previous convictions. From blackmail to embezzlement to cheque fraud, he's done just about everything. He was planning to unload a nice packet of dud notes on you. Know your way around dud notes?"

"I didn't ask you for any information."

"Then why did you keep phoning me? No, Mr Blum, like I said to you only the other day in the Pegasus Bar, the really interesting thing is power. Money or narcotics alone, that's not interesting unless you can convert it into political influence. You can't survive in business these days without politics. Larry, I'll have another little nip."

After his second deep draught, Hackensack's earlobes began to glow. Blum declined the flask with thanks.

"Perhaps you'd like to tell me where you got all this information about me, Mr Hackensack. And what the point of this meeting is."

"Oh, come on, Blum, what's the matter with you? You called in at the firm's offices in Frankfurt . . ."

241

"What's your secretary's first name, by the way?"

". . . you kept phoning and begging us to help you protect your investments."

"Yes, Mr Hackensack – I wanted advice on how to lay it out, on protection. I didn't want it stolen."

"Who said anything about stealing? We kept preventing people from stealing it. What do you think those two charming characters would have done with you and your junkshop?"

"I see. And what are *you* going to do with the cocaine?"

"What you'd have done, Mr Blum. We're going to invest it."

He drew the sample case towards him and opened it. His eyes seemed about to pop out of their sockets, his lips quivered. His nose went as red as if he had just drunk a whole bottle of bourbon straight down. He stared at Blum through his reading glasses.

"What on earth's this?"

"You don't know everything, I see, Mr Hackensack. Good things come in those cans."

42

"And now I'll tell you a little story. A cigar, Larry!"

So Larry was in charge of the Havanas too. Hackensack lit one, made himself comfortable and told the story, or at least as much of it as Blum was supposed to know. They were all sitting around the table smoking now, and Blum was playing with his flick-knife. A good feeling, but that was all. How a former CIA agent, a Flemish missionary and a member of a special Australian commando unit had met up in the last autumn of the Vietnam War, as prisoners of the Vietcong in a war-torn jungle village 250 miles north of Saigon, remained a mystery, unless you fell back on the power of coincidence. The fate they could expect was no mystery. While Hackensack told the tale in his broad accent, the Australian sat back in his armchair staring at the tall double windows with the rain beating against them. Brother Norman had closed his eyes and seemed to be meditating. Blum saw a fly circling above the standard lamp. It had a rather high-pitched buzz, almost like a mosquito. Certain people took their own mosquitoes around with them. Hackensack saw that Blum was not attending very closely, and cut his story short. They had survived back then because each of the three prisoners had a talent that came in useful in such a situation – one had power, one had cunning, the third had faith.

"An everyday story, you see, Mr Blum, everyday for those who were there at the time. But each of the three

243

of us was marked by the experience in a special way – the commando lost a lung, the missionary lost his ability to function in ordinary life, and I – well, I lost principally my reserve funds. So we decided to work together in future, and we did. We brought off a number of little coups. I say little, but some were triumphs that one man alone would never have pulled off. You see, Norman had been with the mission for twenty-five years—"

"Would that by any chance be the Brothers of the Last Days Mission?"

"I see you sometimes do keep your eyes open. Personally, I worked for the government a long time before I branched out into the free economy. Between us we have a good deal of experience. And since Larry's been involved in investigating the drugs trade we've caught some really big fish. Oh yes, my dear Blum, we're on a lucky streak."

He lovingly patted one of the jumbo cans.

"What would you have done if I'd sold the stuff – in Munich or Frankfurt or Amsterdam?"

"Oh, we'd have thought of something. You wouldn't have kept the money in your hands for long."

"But when I was in Munich you still had no idea about it."

"Larry has been after Rossi for quite some time. When you suddenly got mixed up in it, well, of course that upset our plans a little. But then you called us of your own accord. Lucky for you, Blum."

"Lucky for me? You're telling me you'd have got the money away from me, and now you say I was lucky?"

"We're not interested in the money, Blum," Larry put in.

"I can imagine. You all have pretty well-paid jobs, as far as I can tell."

"You really make a useless drugs dealer," said Hackensack equably. "Hopefully that'll dawn on you some time. It really is best to leave the narcotics business to pros and the government these days. So now let me tell you something else. Like Larry just said, we're not so interested in the money. We want to retire, preferably to a country where we can hold the reins ourselves. Everyone dreams of his own little island kingdom where he's the boss, am I right? Well, we've found ours. Ever heard of Abaco?"

Blum stared wordlessly at Hackensack.

"No, that'll have been before your time. I dare say you were still freshening up icons with gold leaf and so on around then. Anyway, Abaco is an island in the Bahamas, and a few years back there was this idealistic millionaire who'd always fancied running his little own state and playing Lord Bountiful there. So he recruited one of our top people to liberate the island from the Bahamas. The plan almost worked, too, only the agent came to grief over Watergate. So the Great Revolution of Abaco never took place. Having your own republic is not just fun, you know – it's very good, lucrative business too. From the stamps to the free port to the casinos. See what I'm getting at?"

Blum lit an HB. His last but one. Time was getting on.

"The only thing that interests me, Mr Hackensack, is why do you need my cocaine?"

"In the place we've picked for ourselves, five pounds of cocaine gives a lot of prestige, Mr Blum. Here you'd just get money for it, out there it'll provide a basis for our coup."

"Really? Then buy the cocaine, Mr Hackensack. You're welcome. I'll give you a good discount too. After all, we've known each other since Malta. Let's say fifty grand. Dollars, of course. Or I'll take any other currency, Mr Hackensack, only it must be in cash. And freshly laundered, if you don't mind."

Hackensack knocked the ash off his cigar. The leather armchair groaned under his weight. "But Blum, we don't need to buy your cocaine now. We already have it."

"Maybe you ought to tell him about the job, Harry," said the Australian.

"Okay. Your performance as a drugs dealer was nothing brilliant, Blum, but of course I realize that these last two weeks do give you a certain right to compensation. And Larry, who knows you better than I do, thinks we could use you in our coup. You look good, you know languages, and I guess something's left over from your activities as an art dealer and a pusher of porn mags. So if you like you can join us."

"As a brother too," said Norman, "don't forget that, Harry, he'd be welcome as a brother too."

Blum stubbed out his cigarette. "Now you listen to me, Mr Hackensack. And you too, brothers. I don't need any job from you, and the hell with your island. You can go to any island, any tiny reef in the world, and it'll be the same old shit. Governments, missions, war. And don't forget plain old robbery with violence. But you don't do it with me. I don't want your power, Hackensack. I don't need a job either, I already have one. I work for Blum and Co. I'm my own firm, my own one-man firm . . ."

"That's not the message your file broadcasts."

"Well, see, that shows what you get unloaded on you these days in the self-service stores. And as for the snow, Hackensack, I don't want compensation for it. It belongs to me. Either I go out of this door with it or you can use it to clean your teeth. Sekt or seltzer water, Hackensack, it's one or the other for me."

"What do you have against me?"

"You want to take my stuff and you ask what I have against you?"

"I'm offering you the chance of your life, man!"

"Really? Where? As what? As breakfast manager on your island of Abaco?"

Hackensack looked at Larry. "I told you, Larry, we really can't use the man."

"You're dead right there," said Blum, standing up. "You can't use me, not for your purposes."

"I'm beginning to see why you never managed to get rid of the stuff anywhere, Blum. The way you carry on ... look, don't make yourself ridiculous. There's no getting around the facts. You had your little chance – it was a tiny one, sure, but it was there – and you didn't know what to do with it. So you just carry on with your porn magazines, your antiques, your butter. You'll see how far that gets you. But the cocaine stays here. I tell you something, regard it as my fee."

"Fee?"

"You wanted me to advise you, and so I have, Mr Blum. The sum of my advice is: close down your firm and go to hell!"

At the door, Blum looked round again. The red cans shone in the light. They'd worn well. But that was as much as he could say about them now.

43

The rain was slackening off. The tide broke on the beach and sprayed foam over the buoys, the pebbles, the sand with the dirt and rubbish on it. The sky was a misty grey with pale patches in it, no stars. Far away the lights of a fishing boat danced on the sea. So here he was on the beach, with the gulls perching on the roof-tops of the hotels where the lights were going out. Blum switched on the torch the sales rep had given him and flashed the beam over the rolling waves. But what message could he send? Nothing had happened to him. Or what had happened to him was what hap-pened to everyone, every day. SOS, that was the mes-sage from every minute spent on land. He threw the torch into the sea. All gone, nothing left of what he had had. He lit his last cigarette. Maybe I ought to light it with my last banknote, he thought, but you're never quite that free. You're still what you always were, you were in luck there, you were what everyone wanted to be, a small-time winner on the long trek between Sekt and seltzer water. A gull began screeching overhead, others followed it, and they raced over the dark waves that were coming closer and closer to Blum as they broke. The sirens of the ferries howled in dock. He heard no footsteps, only the cough slowly approach-ing. Larry stood by him for some time. The light from the street lamps spread far over the beach, but they themselves remained in the shadows. Flecks of foam swirled over the sand. Finally the Australian threw his cigarette butt away. The wind swept it over to the promenade.

"You could still come," called Larry. "I have the tickets."

"I can buy my own tickets."

"Hackensack's a good man!"

"You could say that of anyone."

"And you'd have a good job on the island."

"Peanuts," said Blum, who had been thinking of Mr Haq.

"You're never going to manage on your own!"

"I was managing just fine until you lot came along."

"Islands are getting rare these days, Blum!"

"Too bad."

"Listen, you don't hold that about the magazines against me, do you? It was all part of the job."

"And a bloody miserable job too, Larry."

The Australian did not reply. The waves were lapping over their feet now. Then Larry said, "What will you do now, Blum?"

Yes, what would he do now? Once again he had the problem of choice. Some firms went bust, others carried on. Some people were losers, but that didn't make the rest winners. He threw his cigarette end into the wind and looked at his watch.

"I'm going to see the show at the Roxy Bar," said Blum.

BITTER LEMON PRESS
LONDON

Bringing you the best literary crime and *romans noirs* from Europe, Africa and Latin America.

Thumbprint   *Fredrich Glauser*

A classic of European crime writing. Glauser, the Swiss Simenon, introduces Sergeant Studer, the hero of five novels.

January 2004   ISBN   1–904738–00–1   £8.99 pb

'This genuine curiosity compares to the dank poetry of Simenon and reveals the enormous debt owed by Duerenmatt, Switzerland's most famous crime writer, for whom this should be seen as a template.'   *The Guardian*

Holy Smoke   *Tonino Benacquista*

A story of wine, miracles, the mafia and the Vatican. Darkly comic writing by a best-selling author.

January 2004   ISBN 1–904738–01–X   £8.99 pb

'Much to enjoy in the clash of cultures and superstitions, in a stand-off between the mafia and the Vatican. And a tasty recipe for poisoning your friends with pasta. Detail like this places European crime writing on a par with its American counterpart.' *Belfast Telegraph*

The Russian Passenger   *Günter Ohnemus*

An offbeat crime story involving the Russian mafia but also a novel of desperate love and insight into the cruel history that binds Russia and Germany.

March 2004   ISBN 1–904738–02–8   £9.99 pb

'Simultaneously a road movie adventure, a tight thriller and an elegantly written love story.'   *Der Spiegel*

Tequila Blue   *Rolo Diez*

A police detective with a wife, a mistress and a string of whores. This being Mexico, he resorts to arms dealing, extortion and money laundering to finance the pursuit of justice.

May 2004   ISBN 1–904738–04–4   £8.99 pb

'Diez describes a country torn by corruption, political compromise, and ever-threatening bankruptcy, in poetic but also raw language.'   *L'Humanité*

Goat Song   *Chantal Pelletier*

A double murder at the Moulin Rouge. Dealers, crack addicts and girls dreaming of glory who end up in porn videos.

July 2004   ISBN 1–904738–03–6   £8.99 pb

'She is a wonderful story teller, captures your heart in three short sentences, and takes you through the gamut of emotions, from laughter to tears. A master of funny, bittersweet dialogue. A classic *roman noir* hero, the tired inspector, is completely reinvented by Pelletier.'   *Le Monde*